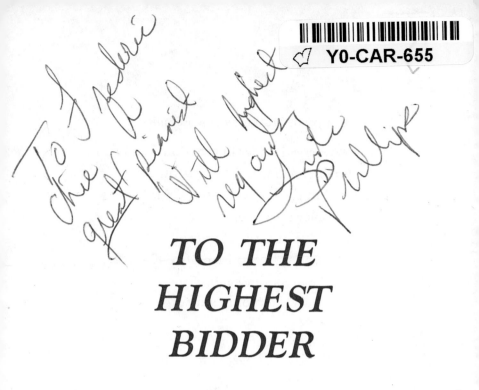

TO THE
HIGHEST
BIDDER

Published in the United States of America by
Newport Literary Society
31 Division Street,
Newport, Rhode Island 02840.
newportlit@yahoo.com
www. newportliterary.org

Library of Congress Cataloging-in Publication Data
Library of Congress Catalog Number: 2003111922

Phillips, Linda.
To the Highest Bidder/Linda Phillips
p.   cm.
ISBN 0-9743556-0-7   13.95

The modern characters in this book are entirely fictional, and any resemblance to real persons is both coincidental and unintentional.

Printed in the United States of America
First Edition

TO THE HIGHEST BIDDER

Linda Phillips

NEWPORT LITERARY SOCIETY
Newport, Rhode Island

Acknowledgements:

This book is respectfully dedicated to the artists and artisans who created the beautiful objects that endure across centuries, and are prized and pursued by men and women of discernment.

It is lovingly dedicated to my children Paige Bart and Richard Fronapfel, Jr.; to my dear friend Jo Sandness; and to Mary Ann Tirone-Smith, novelist and exceptional teacher, in whose class at Fairfield University the dialogue began.

The Cadwalader Chair

The Cadwalader Chair   1770-1771

An exceptional example of American rococo, this opulently carved and upholstered easy chair with "hairy paw" feet was made in the shop of Thomas Affleck (1740–1795). Born and apprenticed in Scotland, Affleck arrived in Philadelphia in 1763, where he became one of the city's most prestigious and successful cabinetmakers. Credit for carving the chair's frame of mahogany, poplar, oak, and white pine is given to James Reynolds, Nicholas Bernard, and Martin Jugiez, carvers Affleck regularly employed; the upholstery of silk damask was done by Plunkett Fleeson. It is regarded as the most grandiose design for an easy chair produced by American craftsmen during the 18th century.

Commissioned by Revolutionary War patriot Brigadier-General John Cadwalader (1742–1786), a prosperous businessman, and his wife Elizabeth, considered the wealthiest woman in America when they were married in 1768, the chair graced their Philadelphia townhouse, one of the grandest homes in the emerging United States. Because members of the Continental Congress were frequent guests of the Cadwaladers, it is quite possible that a George Washington or John Adams sat in this chair while discussing and planning the revolution.

The chair remained in the Cadwalader family until the 1950s. When it turned up thirty years later, its discovery captivated the arts world. Consigned for auction in New York, the chair was acquired in 1987 by collector and trustee of the Philadelphia Museum of Art H. Richard Dietrich, Jr., who in 2002 gave it to the museum on its 125th anniversary.

A surviving bill of sale, covering the period from October 13, 1770, until January 14, 1771, shows that General Cadwalader paid Thomas Affleck 4 pounds, 10 shillings for the easy chair.

Prologue

Philadelphia 1770

The candles guttered as the door of the shop scraped open, admitting wintry air and swirling snow. "If you please, sir, Mistress Reynolds asks you to attend on her, for it's past suppertime," the youth said to his father, rubbing his hands together for warmth. The smell of wood, sawdust, varnish and oils permeated the small cabinet works on Lownes Street.

"Yes, yes, tell your mother I shall be along forthwith," said the craftsman absent-mindedly. His eyes, straining in the growing dark, never left the piece of wood held in the vise before him, and his hands continued the slow, painstaking shaping. Acanthus leaves on a serpentine skirt, certainly worthy of Thomas Chippendale! The chair would be a work of art, the finest in the Colonies, the showpiece of General Cadwalader's splendid new house on Second Street.

His fingers, cramping from the cold, continued the minute motions as tiny shavings fell to the floor.

Few men have virtue to withstand the highest bidder.

—George Washington

Chapter 1

Simon Haden-Jones burst through the double doors of Endicott's into the pale spring sunshine of upper Park Avenue. The headline of *The Wall Street Journal,* tucked carelessly into the pocket of his overcoat, read "Endicott's surpasses Sotheby's in 1986. Rev...First in Centuries-old riva...." The rest was obliterated by the paper's folds. James, the uniformed doorman, was assisting Mrs. Mona Elliott from her limousine.

"Good morning, sir," he said deferentially.

Haden-Jones merely nodded and smiled. He needn't make a fuss over Mrs. Elliott; she was John Bunch's client from Jewelry, not his. At the corner of 72nd Street, he purchased a red carnation from a vendor and put it jauntily through the buttonhole of his topcoat. Then he laughed aloud.

The Chair was his at last. It was going to take a little while to get used to the idea. Wait until he told Freddie.

He turned onto First Avenue, jogging the few blocks to Raffington's, the restaurant frequented by the staff of Endicott's and their clients: sleek, blonde ladies who lunch when in from the Hamptons, their decorators, the odd Arab or Monegasque in town to buy or to do international money dealings, the occasional Eurotrash thrown in for color. The appeal of Raffington's was certainly not in its food, but in its clubby atmosphere, the dark, English-pub-like rooms, and Malcolm, who knew by divine intuition who should be seated where and next to whom.

9

"Mr. Haden-Jones, good to see you today," Malcolm greeted him warmly, as always. "Mr. Trowbridge is already here." He led Simon to his usual table.

"You look like a mongoose who's swallowed something particularly delicious," said Freddie, rolling his absurd eyes. He always wore a Homburg, even indoors; it was his trademark. Rumors in New York's art and auction circles were rampant. Some said that Freddie had a deformed skull. Others that his hair had been singed off in a fire, and his skin scarred and disfigured. The less imaginative said simply that he was bald and vain. Had he been a film star, *National Enquirer* photographers would have lurked on the pavement beneath his 6th floor bathroom window with telephoto lenses. As it was, Freddie Trowbridge (*né* Trosper) was merely the object of endless speculation. He was the French furniture expert at Bronte's, another world-famous auction house and arch rival of Endicott's, Christie's and Sotheby's. He and Simon had met in an interns' class at the Metropolitan Museum of Art, and had liked each other at once. Although Simon had been quite wary at first of Freddie's sexual proclivities, his fears were put to rest immediately. Freddie let him know that he was interested only in friendship, quipping, "I'm mildly corrupt, but discreet." They'd been friends ever since.

"Come on, Simon, spill *les haricots*," Freddie urged. Simon sat down, ordered a Scotch, and breathed deeply.

"I got it. I got the Cadwalader chair," he said, low but triumphant.

"You didn't, did *not!*" Freddie yelped. He sputtered and choked, eyeing Simon with disbelief. "The Peabodys have owned that chair since the late 18th century! They said it would never, ever come on the market. Simon, refresh my memory: Didn't old Nicholas' will expressly state that if the heirs fell into terrible circumstances, or failed to produce issue to put their little rumps upon it, the chair was go to the American Wing of the Metropolitan?

Simon nodded.

"Oh, Simon, did you really acquire it? I mean, tell!"

"Shh—not so loud, Freddie. I'm not ready to announce the acquisition, and the chair's still in the town house in Philadelphia," Simon said.

"God, it's a genuine Thomas Affleck, isn't it?" Freddie was salivating. "How can I stand this? Thank God I'm in French, or I'd be depressed, depressed, *depressed*."

"Freddie, you're the only one I can trust to be truly happy for me," Simon said. "You are, aren't you? And please—not a word until I've arranged for the press announcement."

Freddie nodded. Simon's request was obviously counter to his instincts and impulses. They ordered seafood crepes.

The contrast between the men was startling to the casual observer. Simon was 6' 4", rugged, a former junior tennis champion with a smooth, dark head of hair. Freddie was small, fair and theatrical, flamboyant in dress and language. Sensing that Simon's mind was racing, Freddie made small talk throughout the lunch, intentionally not alluding to The Chair. Over demitasses of thick black coffee, Simon willed himself out of his preoccupation, bringing up the morning's article in the *Journal*. "You saw that we surpassed Sotheby's. It was the Impressionist sale that pushed us over."

"Yes, yes, we at Bronte's just pretend that totals don't exist, since we're not in the running. I'm sure our president has convinced *tous les* employees that the article is merely trompe l'oeil wallpaper, and the figures mere legerdemain. I assume congratulations are in order?"

"It seems so. Well, my friend, what's on for the afternoon?" Simon asked.

"*Is* there an afternoon after your stunning news? Must the rest of us drone on?"

Simon laughed aloud. It helped release his tension.

"Researching provenances...working with photographers on the Delafield sale...the usual. I shall be politely kissing Mrs. van den Meer's ass this evening at six. I'm after her Limoges collection, you know," said Freddie. He paid the check—"my turn"—and they rose from the table. "Cheery-bye, you wretched exploiter of the rich and titled."

"Good-bye, old sport." Simon was smiling as they stood up to leave Raffington's, which pleased Freddie. "See you at the Dunleigh's party on the 6th?" They swung out of the fashionable restaurant.

Freddie nodded assent as he deftly flagged a cab to a stop and opened the door.

"Oh, Simon," he turned back. "Tread carefully. This particular bit of inventory isn't going to make you much-loved and revered by the dealers—or the other experts, either." Freddie seldom spoke seriously, and Simon was taken aback.

"You're quite right," Simon said after a pause.

"And remember," Freddie closed the cab door and spoke through the open window, "all work and no play make Simon a very dull boy." The cab moved into traffic, with Freddie waving a handkerchief in a parody of farewell.

)(O)(O)(

Alex Putnam was on the phone with *Des Artes Magazine* in Paris again, carefully describing a piece of the Duchess of Tudor's jewelry.

"Fifty-three pavé diamonds in a leopard-shaped brooch," he repeated.

Director of Public Relations for Endicott's, Alex received every unclassifiable call, from *The New York Times* antique columnist to the craziest crank threatening to disfigure a

12

painting. Today he felt as if the telephone were a part of his anatomy.

God, would 5:30 ever come! He needed the hour before the medieval paintings reception began downstairs. Needed it more desperately than usual. It was 5:23, and the seconds seemed to be crawling by.

Some nights, Alex thought of Endicott's as a mercantile House of Usher, or as a fabulously inventoried moving and storage company. This night it seemed like a campus, with the various departments—European Paintings, American Furniture, Pre-Columbian Artifacts, English Porcelains—its sororities and fraternities. Ah, college! Sometimes he longed for the good old days at Middlebury.

5:32. Thank God. "Good night, all. Oh, Diana, be sure to take the press release drafts for the fine prints auction to Delbert before the reception. Tha-anks."

He sank into a red damask wing chair, on loan from European furnishings. His office, without windows, was a microcosm of Endicott's, a revolving museum. He regularly borrowed from "the stacks" the pieces he wanted to live with until they came up for auction. Now, as he surveyed the small room, he saw a Gilbert Stuart portrait, some Russian bibelots, and a Simon Willard banjo clock, as well as the marvelous Louis XVI desk. I've not only arrived, he thought, I am ensconced. It's quite a life. But I wish the pressure would let up. He sighed, reached into his pocket for his wallet, took out a crisp $20 bill, and looked at it. You won't buy much in this place, he thought, but you're invaluable to me. Carefully rolling up the bill, he poured out a line of fine white powder onto the priceless desk, and inhaled ecstasy.

Chapter 2

The last three years had been one breathless rush for Selena Fraccese, of the House of Fraccese of Rome and Florence. *Firenze!* When she thought of it, warm fire flowed through her veins, and the passion of art, of centuries of creation, thrilled her. When in the Florence house as a child, she had stared in awe at the remnants of Renaissance architecture, the frescoes, and the articulated 15th century statuary of Michelangelo's period. Now she lay on her bed and stared restlessly at the budding branches outside her dorm room window at Wesleyan University, then abruptly flung herself over onto her back.

Spring bringing us to life again, she thought.

An early spring, thank God! After the long, dark Connecticut winter, her Mediterranean spirit and body longed for sun and the sensual touches of warm air, water, sand. It was hard for her to think clearly; it had all happened very fast. When she learned of the summer apprenticeships open at Endicott's, she'd already planned her summer—a wonderful summer in the south of France and Italy, ending of course in Florence—with Neal. She thought with disbelief: I didn't even know Neal last spring.

Neal, Neal. How could she tell him? How could she make him understand? She wasn't sure that she understood herself. To spend a summer in the heat of New York City among dusty relics doing donkey's work? Oh, no, she was quite certain Neal wouldn't understand. But what would he do? What would he say?

It had been so easy for her. The posting on the bulletin

board in the Art History department read:

**SUMMER INTERNSHIPS AVAILABLE IN
GREEK AND ROMAN ANTIQUITIES,
CONTEMPORARY PAINTINGS, JUDAICA,
AND AMERICAN FURNITURE.**

**APPLY TO: ROBERTA HATCH,
DIRECTOR OF INTERNS**

**ENDICOTT'S
PARK AVENUE
NEW YORK, NEW YORK
—FOUNDED 1752—**

A door opened suddenly in her mind, and she could see beyond it. After a quick mental inventory, she concluded that the most valuable training to her, as a European student, would be in American furniture. In Europe, Italy particularly, American antiques were considered impostures, *arrivistes*. With only two hundred years of history, how could the country boast "antiques"? The Italians threw up their hands.

The moment she had decided to apply, she had taken a felt-tip pen and crossed through the words American Furniture, writing in the margin "filled." As an afterthought, she had wondered how many other universities were displaying the poster. No time for the mail, she had concluded, and immediately placed a person-to-person call to Miss Roberta Hatch, Endicott's, New York City.

A mention of her fellowship, her grade point average, and a confirmation that she was indeed the daughter of the Duce di Fraccese, a minor noble and great patron of the arts, secured her a preliminary promise of the internship.

16

It seemed so right. Except for Neal. Her heart began to pound.

Selena pulled herself off the bed, stood up, shook out her long chestnut hair, and walked to the mirror. The reflection that looked back at her announced her ancestry: the lovely skin and clear blue eyes of her English mother; the dark hair, full lips and strong features of her Italian father. She was tall, reed slim, and moved with the perfect grace of a fine quarter horse. Restless, she began to pace the small room. Another glance in the mirror revealed the apprehension in her eyes.

On happy days, when her appearance pleased her, she thought she had inherited the best of both countries' characteristics. On difficult days, her father's passionate nature coupled with the natural reticence and composure of her mother would war within her. Neal understood this instinctively, usually predicting which traits would prevail, given the nature of the particular situation.

Selena had thought long and hard before coming to an American university, when Paris or London were within easy range and were more logical. As a child, she had been taken to the major museums in all the European cities. She had played in the stairwell beneath the *Winged Victory of Samothrace* at the Louvre, rolled marbles in Amsterdam's Rijksmuseum under Rembrandt's *Night Watch*, and skipped through the small, elegant rooms of London's Tate Gallery, avoiding the modern constructions on the floor. Once, at eight, she'd created a stir at London's Victoria and Albert Museum by disappearing—only to be found by a frantic father, asleep on a comfortable couch in the Constable room.

Yet Selena knew that art was new as well as old, and that creation and preservation always worked in an exquisite counterpoint.

Enough of this. I must face him, she thought, running a comb through her hair and reaching for her jacket and muffler. Neal was probably waiting for her; it was after four. She'd tell him today. She had to.

Selena hurried downstairs to the bicycle rack and set out for Paducci's restaurant, where she and Neal often met. They had to be discreet about being seen together. Professor-student liaisons were particularly frowned upon in the small New England liberal arts schools like Wesleyan. A breath of scandal now for either of them would be disastrous, with graduation only a year off for her, and Neal up for tenure.

She smiled at the thought of his great talent for finding ethnic cafes where he could bring his own wine. The wine collecting was part of the joie de vivre that she found so irresistible in him. It was not so much that he sought pleasure—although he certainly did—as that he experienced almost everything as pleasure, even the exercise of the intellect.

He had deep brown eyes, a well-shaped professorial beard, and dark curling hair. He was not exactly handsome, but well made and magnetic. "Damn, damn, he's just sexy," she admitted to herself as she wheeled her bike into the parking lot and put it into the back of Neal's parked Wagoneer.

Neal had broken open the bottle of Australian cabernet sauvignon. When he saw her, he leaned back in his chair, pushing his long legs out in front of him, and said almost brusquely, "Hi, baby." Only the slight flush and the quick aversion of his eyes gave away the intensity of his feeling. "Where were you?"

"Something came up. I'm sorry." She spoke English with a British accent, occasionally flavored by the lilt of her native Italian. Selena sat down and unwrapped the long, knitted muffler from her neck. Why was she always nervous when she saw him? Her heart raced, and there was some indefinable charge in the air. They kissed lightly.

He poured her wine into the thick tumbler.

"Here, try this. It's got a really complex flavor." Their hands touched as he handed her the glass. "I talked to Sam today about the farmhouse in Provence. He thinks we can stay two weeks in July. It's great—near the wine country and a couple of four star restaurants, if we can afford them by then." Neal smiled and drained his glass.

Selena looked away and took a long draught of the wine. It warmed and steadied her. This was going to be more difficult than she'd expected. Why had she done it, anyway? Madonna, she needed courage.

Neal's knee was resting lightly against hers under the table. She touched it, caressed it a moment, then asked slowly, "What shall we eat?"

"Scungilli," he said, and laughed. He knew she loathed it.

"Let's have tortellini, with cream sauce," she suggested.

"And gnocchi, and pesto bread," Neal urged.

Many Friday afternoons they ate bountifully, drank good wine, made intellectual puns, sparred over Italian literature, laughed heartily, and ended up at Neal's apartment, listening to his enormous collection of records and making love until morning. She thought of it as a little ritual: the wine gave him courage, relaxed him, and the conversation brought them close. Then came the lovemaking. It was the most intense, private, fulfilling, and passionate experience she had ever had, or had ever imagined. Neal was deeply sensual. He always created a heady atmosphere for them in his apartment, lighting incense and candles, and putting on smoky jazz. He loved to look at her. He loved her long legs in tights and high heels, with her chestnut hair piled on her head and held with combs. He took her in visually, as if she were an exquisite painting. He would lie on pillows and let his arousal come slowly, pulling at him, as she undressed, and nude from the waist up, walked, sat, struck playful poses. Then he would touch her, and she would drown in his scent, his skin. The young men Selena had met before Neal were respectful and proper. Neal had been absolutely in command from their first encounter, and could will of her what he wanted on those elemental Fridays. And she feared it was becoming addictive.

This afternoon was different. She couldn't engage in the repartee, couldn't laugh at Neal's outrageous humor, couldn't concentrate on his long, involved story of an instructor, fresh from M.I.T., who was wracking the department's collective nerves.

When they'd finished their food and ordered espresso, Neal fell silent.

"What's wrong?" he asked quietly, taking her hand and kissing her fingers.

Selena's heart rushed, and she drew her hand away. "Could we postpone the trip?"

Neal, suddenly serious, eyed her with total concentration. "Till when?"

"Next summer."

"Next summer? What are you talking about? It's all set."

"I want to accept an internship at Endicott's in American Furniture." The words came out too rapidly.

Neal said nothing, but she knew he was shocked and for once, at a loss for words.

"Why, Selena?" His voice was flat; he was retreating into himself as he always did when he was hurt.

"It's such a wonderful chance, Neal. This is my last summer in the U.S. I must think of my career after I graduate. Endicott's is like the British Museum. They authenticate the world's great art, they are universally known, they are the ultimate authority. Think of what it will mean to have worked there! Think of what I'll learn!" She stopped awkwardly

"What about us?" Neal asked. "What will it mean to us? Did you think about that? We've planned this trip so we could have time together, without hiding and without schedules. I don't understand. Can't you change it?"

"Of course I thought about us. I know we planned to travel, but the trip was more for you, because you wanted to see France and Italy, and because it fitted your schedule. We can go next summer, but I can't go to Endicott's next summer. Come to New York with me and do research."

Neal looked at her steadily, then pushed back his chair and stood up.

"Okay."

"What do you mean, 'okay'?" Selena asked.

"I get the picture. Let's go."

Neal helped her with her jacket. They left Paducci's without speaking, without touching.

"I'll drive you back to the dorm," he said without inflection.

"All right," Selena said, surprised. It hadn't ever been this serious between them before. They climbed into the Wagoneer and rode in silence, her bicycle clanking arrhythymically against the metal door.

When they arrived at the dorm, Neal looked at her for a minute, then said slowly, "I don't like being less important to you than some old furniture."

She couldn't think of anything to say that would be of any comfort to either of them. She got out, retrieved the bike, and walked to the driver's window. He reluctantly rolled it down.

"Neal, it's important to me," she pleaded.

"Bye, Selena," Neal said and drove away. She stood looking after him until the taillights of the Wagoneer grew dim.

Chapter 3

"Hadley Brown had a fit about the chair! They say he hasn't recovered yet." Freddie's glee came through the phone as he described the distinguished dealer's reaction to Simon's coup.

Simon leaned back and put his feet up on his desk.

"Yes, I've had dozens of calls," Simon said. "I'll never get used to the power of *The New York Times*. Oh—*Antiques* magazine has called, and Alex tells me that *House & Garden* wants to do a feature on me and my flat. It seems like a lot of horseradish. But I'll do it if it will help the chair sell."

Simon had expected a tempest in the little teapot of the antiques world, but what he was reaping was more like a firestorm—or a firebombing.

"Good God, Freddie, even the Horace Collection now seems quite mild by comparison." Simon referred to the acquisition that had made his reputation and secured his post at Endicott's. "How did they take it over at Bronte's?"

"Oh, Jack's fit to die, and jealous as a jilted mistress—but when isn't he?" Freddie replied. "It's the hairy paws, Simon. Bronte's simply hasn't had any hairy paw furniture in years. I keep telling Jack we're still British-owned and you're not, but he's not consoled. Ugly American stepchild, and all that." Freddie cackled, glad that his friend had one-up on his Bronte's counterpart.

"Incidentally, I hear through the grapevine that there's a lot of crossover interest in your chair. They're literally coming out of the woodwork! The Dunleighs are sniffing. So is that Wall Street couple who built that monstrosity of a

23

house in Southampton and are trying to fill it with *anything*. That recluse of a developer who owns the air rights to every other building in Manhattan—what's his name? *And*—are you seated, my friend?—Mona Elliott wants your hairy-pawed throne." Freddie paused for effect.

"Mona Elliot! She hasn't bought anything but jewelry in years. Why the Cadwalader?"

"It seems that your chair is becoming a *chose celebre* or something, Simon, though God knows why. It's like the Hope Diamond or the Holy Grail. Only one seeker can own it, and will they all be vying!"

"What about the museums? Have you heard anything?"

"The bucks, Simon, the bucks. Hard for any museum to run in this race," Freddie said thoughtfully.

"I thank you for the information, Freddie. Funny—this is one time when the Japanese and Arabs aren't so interested. This is strictly Yankee Doodle and Stars and Stripes. What a business we're in, my friend." Simon gave a long sigh.

"You've spoken volumes, Simon. Enjoy it while it lasts. After the sale, it will be as ancient history. Of course, you'll do *Antiques*, and of course you'll admit *House & Garden*. I'm actually jealous. They've never asked to feature Trowbridge Manor. Well, cheery bye for now." Freddie rang off.

Simon pulled his legs from his desk and swiveled around in his chair. The furor occasioned by the Cadwalader chair had taken so much of his time that the smaller collections and his department's submissions for the boutique auctions were suffering. He was behind. He needed to spend some time with Mike O'Donnell in appraisals, and with his assistant who was writing descriptions for the catalogues. He needed an intern. And now he was late for a guest appearance at a board of directors meeting in Endicott's private dining room—a high honor indeed.

Simon couldn't wait for the balky elevator, so he took the

stairs from the fourth to the second floor, two at a time. He passed the Brancusi sculpture in the stairwell, and ran along a corridor lined with prints of the Picassos and Degases which Endicott's had auctioned. What a place, he thought with pride, what a marvelous, marvelous place!

)()()(

E. Martin Wunnicke, Chairman of the Board of Endicott Enterprises, Inc., greeted Simon with a nod as he entered the exquisitely appointed dining room suite. At the far end of the Hepplewhite table was a picture window overlooking the auction floor where preparations were underway for the afternoon session. Telephones were being carried in, and five boards to show figures in five separate currencies simultaneously were being set in place. Harris Tompkins, the auctioneer, incongruous in his tuxedo, chatted casually with an early arrival.

Simon sat in the corner and listened to the business discussion. Endicott's was soaring since its acquisition in 1982 by Wunnicke Industries of Kansas City. The business principles that had made Wunnicke a billionaire in trucking and commercial warehousing somehow were working in the eccentric and scholarly world of the art auction house.

There were six men and one woman in the room. The air of power and influence was palpable, rarefied. They all seemed to move in ether. Simon had interrupted a discussion of the profitability of the boutique auctions that were created for good, usable items that weren't museum or collection quality.

"Are we agreed, then, on Sarah's proposal that we limit items for the boutiques to a minimum appraisal value of $1,000?" Wunnicke asked.

There was a general mumble of consent.

"Thank you, gentlemen; we are agreed. Sarah, please notify all departments of the change, effective immediately. And thank you for the projections. Your work has been invaluable." Wunnicke gave her a guileless smile.

Endicott's Vice President Sarah Dean, M.B.A., nodded to Wunnicke without looking up. She didn't want to fuel the rumors that were afoot about how she got Wunnicke's ear, nor cause a ripple in the gentlemanly board meeting about her own ambitions. Expression of her appreciation of Wunnicke's remarks could come later, in private.

Simon listened to the proceedings with his usual measure of remove, and fought down the sensation of distaste which rose in him whenever he encountered the "others," as he thought of the board of directors and the financial staff.

"I've asked Haden-Jones to join us today," Wunnicke announced, nodding at Simon. "You've probably heard that Simon got the Catwaller chair for us, a fine piece of American furniture, and a major attraction for his department. Bronte's, Phillips, and all the big dealers on Madison and on 57th Street had approached the family before without any luck whatsoever. Simon, we don't know how you did it. Do the Peabody's have a pretty young daughter?"

There was laughter around the table. Simon flushed uncomfortably, thinking back to the circumstances of his acquiring the Horace Collection. Well, people have long memories, particularly for gossip in high places, Simon concluded. Let it pass.

"Thank you, Mr. Wunnicke, for your kind invitation." Simon rose, speaking in his most professional manner. "As you gentlemen know, it is the policy of the experts at Endicott's to seek and to find the finest and most desirable works and collections on earth, and to bring them to the widest possible international attention. When a unique piece like the Cadwalader chair comes to us, it does several

26

important things: It imprints our reputation as the finest auction house in the world, it attracts the most discriminating clientele and collectors to us, and it most certainly generates world-wide publicity."

The Baron Tadeusz Laszlo-Mozinski, who appeared to be asleep, suddenly coughed loudly and fingered his gold-handled cane. His eyes flicked open, and fixed on Simon with profound disinterest.

Simon waited politely. The baron's eyes closed again, and he continued. "There is no longer just a small coterie of buyers of antique furniture. As Mr. Wunnicke so clearly recognized, competition for fine art and antiques is at a fever pitch, given the volatility of other investments. It is our mission—or crusade, if you will—to stand for the peerless, to authenticate and market masterpieces. It's also a great personal satisfaction to me to bring to Endicott's and our clients the rare and the priceless." Simon paused, realizing he was getting carried away again. What's the use, he thought inwardly. They sit there in their Arnold Sulka handmade shirts and Gucci shoes, thinking about their money and their pleasures. They know nothing of art, they care nothing about art. This is a little charade we play out for Wunnicke so that we can have what we want: They get their prestigious directorship, and I keep my job.

"Speaking of priceless, Simon, what is your best guess about the selling price of the Catwaller?" Wunnicke smiled expectantly. His hobby was collecting erotica, and because of his wealth and his ownership of Endicott's, some of it was very fine, although that was quite by accident. His only interest in the other objects that passed through Endicott's doors was the price they would bring at auction. It was all a terrific game to him: Monopoly on a cosmic scale.

The members of the board were at instant attention. All eyes (except Mozinski's, of course) were trained on Simon, particularly Sarah Dean's.

"Mike O'Donnell hasn't seen it yet, and of course we have to strip the upholstery and authenticate the frame. But a good early estimate would be $700,000–900,000," Simon said with justifiable pride.

"Well, it's no Mo-nay, is it," Wunnicke replied after some thought, "but that's a nice piece of change for one item. You're seeing that Alex gets you a lot of press on this one?"

Simon nodded.

Wunnicke stood up and pushed back his chair, a signal that Simon's command performance was at an end.

"Have some coffee, Simon," Wunnicke suggested genially. The board members broke into small groups and were conversing quietly, or helping themselves to charlotte russe at the Georgian sideboard.

"Thank you, no, Mr. Wunnicke. My department is quite busy just now," Simon replied. "I'll be getting back. But thank you for the opportunity to speak to you, and if there are any questions, I'm always available."

As Simon, relieved, left the dining room, Wunnicke walked to the picture window and surveyed the auction floor, followed by Sarah Dean.

"I like that young man, Sarah. Got one hell of a head on his shoulders, and he's a worker. What're they selling down there this afternoon? "

"Clocks and timepieces, Martin."

"Well, let me know when that sale I'm interested in, you know, that Far Eastern stuff with the statue, is coming up." Wunnicke referred to a particularly rare Chinese erotic sculpture. "I'm going to put in a bid on that one."

Suddenly, there were two sharp raps on the table. The baron slowly opened his eyes, fixed them on Wunnicke, and said imperiously, "There will be only one bidder for the Chinese statue, Martin."

Chapter 4

"Whaddya, fucking crazy, girlie?" You ain't gettin' into my cab with that thing!" The cabdriver pointed an accusing finger at the curb where a plastic-wrapped futon sat in a forlorn heap.

"But I'll load and unload it myself," Selena said with unassailable logic. At this, the cabbie looked merely skeptical.

"Look, I have a piece of rope. I'll tie it on top."

The cab accelerated quickly and sped off up Third Avenue.

"At least he speaks English," Selena said to no one in particular.

Addressing the problem of the thirty blocks between the store and her apartment and the bulk of the futon, Selena saw no immediate solution. However she folded the bundle, it wasn't possible to carry it without staggering under its shifting weight.

Suddenly a wave of despair washed over her. Everything in this huge, inhospitable, nightmarish city was like the futon: unmanageable, overwhelming, and maybe impossible.

"No, no, I'll not give in. After all, *I* am a Fraccese," she reminded herself, and struggled again to shoulder the unmanageable pink bundle.

A laughing couple passed her as she tried to pull the futon onto her back, the end dragging like a train. At the corner the couple turned and looked back at her, conferred quickly, and returned.

"Having some trouble?" the young man asked.

"Oh, yes, I am," Selena admitted.

"Where you going?" the girl asked.

"To First Avenue and 83rd," Selena said.

"Okay, we can give you a lift. We've got the company van," the young man said.

"Are you sure? I can pay you...." Selena was apprehensive. Her father had told her many cautionary tales of New York, and what might befall a young girl alone. But one look at the futon, and the memory of last night spent on the hard wood floor, overcame her fears. She nodded. "Hey, that's all right." The two lovers giggled and clasped hands again.

She thought of Neal.

The three of them managed to heft the futon like a mammoth tricorn, and carry it the half block to the green van emblazoned with the motto of Shecky's Pizza—"It Ain't Matzo"—and a large picture of Shecky himself holding a slice.

"The Boss," the young man explained.

As they wedged the futon into the back of the van, the couple introduced themselves as Julio and Loretta.

"I'm an actor—this is just to pay the rent," Julio explained.

"He's *wonderful*," Loretta sighed.

Selena introduced herself.

"Italian, eh?" Julio asked.

"Yes—and English." Selena started as she realized how wonderful it was just to speak normally to someone. In her two days in New York she'd been pushed, shoved, cursed at, importuned, ignored, charged, and propositioned. Maybe there was hope.

"I'm so grateful to you," Selena began.

"Ah, forget it. We all need a break sometimes." Julio smiled broadly.

Loretta sat between them in the front seat as Julio maneuvered the van into traffic.

"I'm a design student at F.I.T. (Selena looked uncomprehending.) The Fashion Institute of Technology," Loretta explained shyly. "Are you a student?"

"I've come to intern at Endicott's Auction Galleries for the summer," Selena explained.

Julio gave a low whistle. Loretta's eyes opened wide. "Endicott's! Boy, are you lucky! What I wouldn't give! How'd you get that?" Loretta's words came out all at once.

The memory made Selena want to laugh and cry at the same time.

"I applied from Wesleyan last spring."

"That's great! Good luck," Julio said. "Hey, when I'm a famous movie star, I'll come to Endicott's and buy all my furniture from you, okay?"

"Okay," Selena agreed happily.

Julio wove skillfully in and out of traffic, crossing to First Avenue at 79th. Loretta talked about her dreams of becoming a world-class fashion designer. She had wedded burlap to spandex for a completely new look in sportswear, and was working on a line of hats done with feathers from the pigeons of New York, freely available in every park. Although it was hard for Selena, brought up on the haute couture of Italy and Paris, to envision those creations, she knew that there was vigor and originality in Loretta's ideas, and that New York, for all its ugliness, spawned such avant-garde creativity.

"We're here," Julio said as he brought the van to a very abrupt halt. Selena was sorry to have to leave them.

"It will be my pleasure to entertain you for dinner as soon as I'm settled," she said.

"You bet! We'll come over some night when I'm not in a play, and Lorrie doesn't have class." Julio turned on the radio and the music of "Prince" blared down the street, commingling with the noise of honking horns, buses

31

starting up, a jackhammer.

"Just call Shecky's and ask for Julio."

Selena could have kissed this improbable knight-errant. He hauled the futon out the van for her, depositing it on the sidewalk.

"You gonna be okay now?" he asked.

She nodded.

"Well, then, see you, Miss Selena of Endicott's."

Loretta smiled and waved as the van, late become a tabernacle of rock music, moved away down the street.

Miss Selena of Endicott's.

XOXOX

Dusk came to the city. A yellow haze enveloped the buildings as the sun sank lazily, making elongated geometric shadows on the brownstones across the street from Selena's small apartment. People hurried home from their jobs in the glass towers, carrying attaché cases. A deliveryman pedaled his bike slowly, unsteadily balancing three bags of groceries in the bent wire basket.

Selena gazed at the scene, enraptured, pushing her hair behind one ear. Yes, there was a rough beauty here. She had done it. She had come. She could manage it alone, without help from her influential family, and without *him*.

And yet, and yet....

Neal—where was he just now? On the plane with the laughing group of musicians with whom he'd decided to tour France and Italy? At home in his apartment packing? Did he miss her terribly, too? Or at all? She didn't know his schedule, certainly not his mind, or his exact itinerary. It hadn't seemed possible to ask that last evening, and he had not offered.

She had finally rung him in early May.

32

"Neal, it's Selena. May we talk?" she'd begun.

"Sure."

"Are you still upset with me? Why haven't I seen you?" she asked feelingly.

There was a long silence.

"I really don't want to talk about it," Neal said.

"Did you think about New York at all?" She felt indecorous bringing it up.

"Selena, look. We can't discuss this over the phone."

"I'll meet you."

"All right," he agreed with reluctance.

"At Paducci's?" she suggested.

"Not there," Neal said quickly. "Look, come on over."

"I'll be there in twenty minutes," she said.

She remembered rushing frantically to put on her most becoming sweater, jeans, and the boots he particularly loved. If he was going to let her go, she was not going to let it be easy for him.

The meeting was strained. Even though Selena quite consciously lured Neal into bed, and made love with him hungrily, he was still distant, closed up. Their nakedness was only physical. He told her that he thought he was in love with her, but couldn't handle her independence, her willful behavior. He suggested that they "take the summer off" from each other, and "see how they felt" when they came back to campus in the fall.

She left him, confused and, in her mind, cheapened. After that evening, she had only glimpsed him occasionally on campus, coming and going. He always nodded perfunctorily.

Could so much have become suddenly nothing? Selena felt as if the sands under her had shifted, and there was no solid place on which to stand, nothing to grasp. It went deeper than pain. She had been wounded in her deepest being.

Still, she ached for him in the New York dusk.

Turning from the darkening vista, she took a small notebook from her book bag. Sitting cross-legged on the futon, she opened it to the page titled "Haiku," and wrote:

"Neal"
I run entangled
In sweet green moss and desire
Whenever you ask.

Chapter 5

Henry Grenfell sat sipping his breakfast tea and staring at *The New York Times* spread on the table before him. He read and reread the fine print of the antiques column and began to mutter, "It's not right. It's not right." Pushing back his chair, harrumphing, and arching his bushy white eyebrows, he walked to the closet, flung open the door, and selected the splendid scarlet coat from its depths.

XOXOX

Selena had chosen a tan linen Armani skirt and an ecru silk blouse for the first day at Endicott's, discarding her Wesleyan dresses as too bohemian for New York. Fearful and eager all at once, she hurried along First Avenue. It wouldn't do to be even a minute late. Beginnings often foretold endings, she believed absolutely.

Turning a corner, she saw the imposing glass double doors of Endicott's, festooned with brass. A uniformed doorman was ushering in the people she didn't yet know, who nodded to each other, or, preoccupied with the day's schedule, stared straight ahead, proceeding with absolute purpose.

She took a deep breath. "All right. I'm all right. It's what I wanted, and I'm going to do my best." She joined the flow of people.

James nodded to her, smiling, opening the portal. "Good morning, Miss."

"Good morning," Selena said, and she stepped through

the doors into that other world.

A curved staircase ran obliquely up to her right, carpeted in heavy grey plush. Looking around hungrily, she saw a filigreed balustrade lined with vases of tall silk flowers; steps to the left, down to a lower level, where she could see paintings hanging, lighted by individual picture lights; a passageway and windows along the front wall to her immediate right leading to what appeared to be an elevator. Not wishing to betray indecision, she started along the corridor.

Immediately, a security guard materialized from a small doorway in the passage. "May I help you, Miss?" Terry O'Donoghue said with a hint of a brogue. Selena noted the intercom strapped to his belt.

"Yes, please. I'm a new summer intern, and I'm looking for Miss Hatch." She was startled by the sudden appearance of the guard. They must be everywhere, she thought, with all the priceless art going in and out, but unless something was amiss, she surmised that they were seldom seen at all.

"Take that elevator there to the third floor reception, and ask for Personnel. If it's working this morning, that is," O'Donoghue advised.

Selena entered the tiny elevator, which lurched unsteadily under her weight. A beautifully groomed young man, blonde with horn rimmed glasses, a bow tie and red suspenders dashed in just as the elevator doors were closing.

"*Just* made it. It takes an hour to come down again, you know," he said to her and the air, pressing the button for four and smoothing back his impeccable hair. Then he shook open his morning *Times* and focused his complete attention on page one.

On the first floor, O'Donoghue was speaking into the intercom. "Mack, looks like the interns are coming in. Going to be one of those days."

36

Selena stepped out on three, and the doors closed behind her, obscuring the rapt young man. She wondered fleetingly who he was. Now facing the front of the building, she noticed the apartment houses across the street, the gaiety of their canopies, the varied and beautiful window treatments, so unlike those of her own modest summer digs. She turned and saw a desk and two glass cubicles.

No one was yet in attendance, so she sat down on the sofa and picked up a copy of *Contemporanea* magazine, but she didn't really read. She was alert to movement, doors closing down the corridors, a laugh wafting up the stairwell. "Hilareee! Coffeee!" a high-pitched voice called out.

The door behind the reception desk opened, and a blonde girl—tailored, soigné, and haughty—swept through and sat down. The elusive Hilary? Selena wondered. The girl ignored Selena utterly, and busied herself with arranging things in drawers. Minutes passed in silence.

It was a standoff. Selena sat uncomfortably. The girl looked everywhere but at her.

Selena finally stood up and cleared her throat.

"Yes?" the girl said without interest.

"Roberta Hatch, please."

"Do you have an appointment?"

"Not exactly, but she's expecting me. I'm a new intern."

"Oh." The girl looked as if she'd discovered something unpleasant floating in her soup. "Name, please?"

Still there was no eye contact with the remote girl. Perhaps she believes that her soul will be compromised, will be pulled right through her eye sockets, Selena thought, smiling wickedly.

"Selena Fraccese."

"Frah-Chay-Zee," the girl jotted. "One moment."

She isn't any older than I am, thought Selena. She looks like one of those young things chronicled in *Details* or *Scene*.

I thought the photographers made them up.

"Through the door, first left to Personnel," the girl said. Selena walked to the door and waited to be buzzed in. There was a lock, activated by push buttons. She guessed that it was done by combination as well as a buzzer. As the buzzer sounded, she opened the door and was reminded of Alice stepping through the looking glass. Here was yet another reality entirely: a warren of corridors through dingy tan walls, filing cabinets stuck in every available space, and—she realized after a few steps—no sunlight at all. Fluorescent bulbs burned behind panels in the ceilings. She passed a bulletin board listing concerts, apartment sublets, Endicott's Calendar of Receptions. The contrast with the luxury and serenity of the public floors was almost shocking. "I am behind the looking glass. But the people in front see only their own glittering reflections."

She turned and walked through a dingy, unmarked door. A young woman seated in what appeared to be a hall said, "Miss Fraccese? Through the next door for Miss Hatch."

Selena said her thanks and went in, finding at last a friendly woman, who got up from behind a large desk and extended her hand.

"Selena. Welcome. Sit down. There will be eight of you coming on board this summer, five women, three men. We'll have an orientation meeting in the lower gallery after lunch, at two. We're very short-staffed, so you'll be asked to do just about everything in your department. Let's see, you're in (she riffled through some file cards) American Furniture. Mr. Haden-Jones. He's very good, you'll learn a lot. I suppose you know about the Cadwalader chair?"

Selena nodded, happy she had read the "Antiques" column of *The New York Times* the preceding Friday. Although her original reasoning for applying in American Furniture had nothing to do with a major acquisition

38

passing through the auction process during her tenure, it would be fascinating to observe. She was pleasantly excited.

Perhaps she could assist in the preparation of the chair for auction. She guessed that it was the equivalent of the *Mona Lisa* to Endicott's American Furniture department.

"Mr. Haden-Jones may have a moment to speak to you if you go up right now." Miss Hatch glanced at her watch, ran her hand through her short dark hair. "He's on four—I'll call ahead. Meanwhile, have my secretary, Ellen, take your photo for your I.D. card. You'll need it to get in here, and also to visit the New York museums. We have reciprocal privileges for employees. ('Employees', Selena thought with pleasure.) Good luck." The efficient Miss Hatch turned her attention to a ringing telephone.

Ellen, equipped with a Polaroid camera, directed Selena to stand against a blank tan wall, and then took a photo in which Selena looked startled, like an exotic fawn. "Your card will be ready this afternoon. You can pick it up it at the interns meeting. Good luck."

Selena retraced her steps, passing by haughty Hilary, and walked to the elevator. No light went on when she buzzed. She saw a staircase to the left, and chose it, disregarding an elongated modern metal sculpture extending from the landing on the third floor to the fourth. Yet another blonde manned the fourth floor reception area, like the third but without the glass cubicles.

"Yes?"

"I'm here to see Mr. Haden-Jones." Selena was beginning to feel increased anticipation and a sense of belonging as she penetrated further into the maze of Endicott's.

"Name?"

"Fraccese. I'm the new intern."

"Go in. It's all the way down the hall." Again, the set-in-aspic demeanor.

Once again the buzzer, the plunge from light to darkness, the long dingy corridor, which she traversed. A young man in shirtsleeves and tie raced along the corridor and swept by her. "Excuse *me*," he intoned, not breaking stride.

The corridor was very long, running the depth of the building. At the end she saw doors on the left and right. She chose the left, and knocked lightly.

"Come in," said a man's deep voice.

She opened the door to a small, beautiful room, with a fine desk of the Federal period centered on a deep red-and-blue Persian rug. Her first impression of Simon was of a smooth, dark head, one strand of hair lying loose, bent over papers, a quill pen poised in one hand. Again, she felt she had entered yet another in a series of strange realms.

"Mr. Haden-Jones?"

Simon looked up—and everything simply stopped, as if he was suspended in time. He didn't breathe, he didn't move. He looked at Selena and blinked, as if he had emerged from pitch darkness into brilliant sunlight. He passed his hand over his eyes once. The light from his lamp shone on her lovely young face, the face from his portrait, exact in every detail. After a long moment's astonished stare, during which he imagined himself walking to her, will-less, and stroking her chestnut hair, he recovered himself and found his voice.

"Er...yes?" He knew he sounded like an idiot.

"I'm Selena Fraccese, the summer intern," she said, stepping to the desk and extending her hand.

"Yes, of course. Well, sit down or something."

"Thank you."

"The new intern, eh? Yes, well. We'll be quite busy while you're here, and I'm afraid you'll have to pitch in with typing letters, filing and the like." He felt as if he were inviting Helen of Troy to do his laundry.

"That will be fine," Selena said.

40

"We have a major piece in the department just now that we're preparing for auction in the fall."

"Yes, the Cadwalader chair." Selena said.

"Oh, you know about it. Good, good...."

There was an awkward pause.

Selena thought it odd that he didn't look at her, but kept fiddling with his pen and a button on his cuff.

"May I assist with the chair?" Selena asked.

She is respectful, Simon thought; I hope she doesn't call me "Sir."

"Certainly, certainly. Have Arabella take you back to the vault this morning to look at it."

Another awkward pause.

"Well, I have a meeting. Welcome—we hope you'll have a rewarding summer. I'll send Arabella in to get you started."

Simon fairly tore out of his office, averting his eyes from the vision in his visitor's chair. Lord, she's so beautiful, and so young; I know now how Dante felt when he first saw his Beatrice, he thought.

Selena waited for Arabella—another indifferent blonde?—and mused: What a strange man. He's young to be such a stuffed shirt.

✕✕✕✕

At the precise moment Simon's gaze first fell on Selena, Henry Grenfell boarded the First Avenue bus at 21st Street. Although the bus was crowded, no one sat within two seats of him, or stood anywhere near him. Amid hushed whispers, a small boy pointed and said, "Look, Mom, look!" but his mother silenced him quickly, and pulled him into the stairwell of the bus' back door, ready to leap off at the first sign of trouble.

XOXOX

"Publicity photos? I don't know anything about any publicity photos." Silently trying to imagine "what next?" Terry O'Donoghue looked at the resplendent figure of Henry Grenfell dressed as a redcoat, complete with powdered wig, white breeches, gold braid, and a musket.

"I'll call Mr. Putnam. Wait here, please."

As O'Donoghue turned his back, Henry Grenfell rushed up the curving stairs, knocking over a vase with his musket. "I'm here on official business of His Majesty, King George III!" he thundered. "Where is the Cadwalader chair?"

"Jesus, Mary and Joseph," muttered O'Donoghue to himself, instantly alert and fumbling for his intercom. "Jesus, Mary and Joseph!"

Chapter 6

Henry stood atop the staircase, surveying the scene below: the security guard mumbling into something black, two grey-haired women looking up at him with amusement. He had breeched the enemy line, but not without cost. Secrecy was impossible now. He must use cunning and speed to find his objective and secure it for his king.

Behind him on the broad landing were a counter displaying art books and Endicott's sale posters, two imposing double doors, and a narrow passageway beyond the counter. "The straight line to the objective is to be used whenever possible," his general had said. Using his musket butt, he pushed open the double doors and flung himself into a smart double-time march down the center aisle of the main auction gallery, where a morning sale was in progress. Heads turned to follow his progress.

That must be their commander, he thought, as he spied the imposing figure at the podium, speaking to an intent audience. But what are those odd paddles they carry? Some new kind of shield, perhaps? Yes, that must be it.

Really, these dealers are becoming awfully eccentric in their dress, Harris Tompkins thought to himself, not missing a beat as he solicited bids on a pair of Louis XVI armchairs.

Henry kept advancing until he was directly under Harris' podium, and the auctioneer felt the first small thrill of alarm. Why hadn't this strange man taken a seat?

"Sir, the Cadwalader chair, if you please. And quickly."

Henry's clipped voice was commanding, and Harris was a little unnerved. He looked straight at Henry and said, "This is the French furniture sale, sir, and if you'll just take a seat, we'll continue."

Henry was having none of it. He pointed his musket directly at the auctioneer, pulling back the hammer. "The Cadwalader chair, sir."

At that moment, two guards appeared at the double doors, and Henry, agile as a cat, darted to the side of the gallery and disappeared behind the velvet curtains.

A low murmur broke out in the audience, and a shaken Harris banged his gavel to restore order.

"Ladies and gentlemen, *just* a little entertainment to remind you of our upcoming sale of English furniture, ha-ha. Now, where were we? The gentleman over there, the bid is $54,000 against you. Do I hear 56?" My God, I hope he doesn't come back, Harris thought. This sale is hard enough. They're all sitting on their fat paddles this morning. What in blazes is going on?

Henry trotted quickly through the corridors of the second floor, alert for guards. His first try at penetration was a blind alley, ending at a locked door. Backtracking, he saw a large freight elevator to his left, marched to it, and pushed the button. He was lucky. It arrived empty, and guessing that he needed to go up, he entered and pushed the button for four.

"Hey, man! Halloween isn't till October." Laughter followed as two moving men, lounging at the fourth floor landing, caught sight of Henry. Between them was a large crate, from which a crystal chandelier was suspended.

With utter dignity, Henry answered the mover, "I'm here for the film about the Cadwalader chair."

"The wha'?"

"The American antique chair," Henry explained. His control was exquisite, and he was pleased with his own

44

daring and quick-wittedness behind enemy lines. This was a mission of glory, the one he'd been waiting for all his life.

"Well, American Furniture department's over there, but I don't know nuthin' about a movie." The moving man hitched up his coveralls and turned his attention to the task at hand. "Come on, Rufe; let's get this chandelier to the loading dock."

Henry walked briskly in the direction the movers had indicated. There simply was no time to waste. The guards knew about his infiltration, and would be in hot pursuit.

He reached the end of the corridor and saw, on the other side of a floor-to-ceiling wire mesh wall, an incredible jumble of objects: chairs, two bonnet-top highboys, dozens of oil paintings that to him looked primitive and flat of perspective. Shelves were crammed with pewter candlesticks, ornate and plain silver, clocks and dishes. He had happened upon the storage area, and felt in his bones that the chair must be somewhere near. But where? To Henry's racing mind, these stacks offered opportunities for concealing himself, as well as proximity to his objective. He swept his eyes along the wire mesh until he spotted a thick, vertical metal bar, indicating a door.

He couldn't believe his good fortune! As he touched it, the door swung open, and he could see a key still in the lock. God favored his mission; that was perfectly clear to him now. He was feverish with anticipation. Moving stealthily through the narrow corridors inside the wire mesh enclosure, he was again amazed by what he saw. The wealth of objects, the sheer number of things dazzled his eyes.

Suddenly he stiffened. There were voices, two of them, high-pitched. He crept silently along the passage and peered cautiously around the last shelf, and there it was, exactly as pictured in *The New York Times*: the Cadwalader chair. It was inside another enclosed area, and two young women were

45

looking at it, one stooped down, touching an elaborately carved foot.

XOXOX

Simon heard the insistent ringing of his telephone, and he sprinted down the fifty feet of corridor, grabbed the receiver from the wrong side of the desk, and irritably said, "Yes?"

"Sir, we have an emergency. This is O'Donoghue from security. Some nut dressed up in a red uniform is running around, yelling that he wants that chair you've got up there—the Cadwalter? I'm sorry, but he got past me and ran up the stairs and through the auction. I've got every guard in the place looking for him, but I wanted you to know. Oh, and Mr. Haden-Jones—he's got some kind of old gun."

Dropping the telephone receiver and letting it dangle, Simon ran from his office and raced toward the locked vault in the storage area, his heart in his throat. His biggest fears had always been theft or accidental breakage, although maniacs had been known to deface paintings at Endicott's by slashing the canvases or throwing acid. He couldn't think of what a fanatic might do to a piece of furniture, but he knew enough to take the situation quite seriously.

He saw Arabella's key protruding from the lock on the door to storage—*damn that girl—why couldn't she be more careful—I've told her a hundred times*—and suddenly felt real fear. He edged quietly through the storage area, aware of a woman's voice speaking softly. As he came around the corner, he saw a remarkable sight and stopped, transfixed.

There on the floor of the vault was the beautiful intern Selena, holding a foot of the Cadwalader chair, and speaking in a calm voice to a tall man dressed—My God!—as a redcoat. For some reason, Simon's mind kept registering the man's spats and his white wig. Yet there was something else, something amiss. What was it?

As he crept closer, he saw Arabella, frozen with terror, standing motionless against the side wall. He advanced slowly, putting a finger to his lips to implore silence. He wasn't sure whether or not Selena could see him. She was looking straight into the eyes of the costumed man, speaking quietly. He could just make out her words..."my father feels the same way as you. You know about King Cadwalader of England? Well, of course, you must. He ruled in the sixth century, and when I told my father about the Cadwalader chair, he said anything that old and precious from King Cadwalader's reign should be in a museum, not be auctioned." Suddenly, Simon knew what was wrong. He saw Henry's musket, the barrel dipping as he listened to Selena. He lunged forward with a strength born of desperation.

)(O)(O)(

"Well, well, and how's my favorite whiz kid this morning?" Wunnicke gave Sarah Dean's shoulder an avuncular pat as he entered her glass-enclosed office, one of four in the executive compound, which was on the second floor of Endicott's, across from the private dining room.

"Fine, thank you, Martin. And how were things in Kansas City?"

"Oh, good, good. Herbert Kazin was there for a meeting—that man's a retailing genius, Sarah. You know, he's figured out the psychology of every technological innovation that stores are using right now in shopping malls. Didn't know the first thing about how to do things, just knew what to do, and hired the right people to design it. I've asked him to join the board here—give those la-dee-da boys a pinch in the pants. Wonder what they'll make of the pair of us in Lon-

47

don?" Wunnicke chuckled heartily. In England, Endicott's was still considered an institution on a par with The British Museum, and an unassailable authority on the authenticity and valuation of antiques.

Sarah smiled enigmatically, and thought: So he thinks Herbert Kazin is a genius? He'll see. He'll see just who's the genius around here.

"Now, Sarah"—Wunnicke settled himself into a chair and unbuttoned his vest—"tell me how you see things here at Endicott's." This was his favorite opening remark, a ploy that enabled him to evaluate the thinking processes of those who worked for him more surely than any psychological test.

Sarah was suddenly center stage, with the glare of a million spotlights on her. She'd been waiting for this day, and she had done her homework—oh, what homework she'd done! Even the brilliant orals she had delivered for her Harvard M.B.A. couldn't hold a candle to the performance she was about to give.

"Martin"—she ruffled a stack of papers for effect—"one of Endicott's major problems has been the reserves. When the owner sets a minimum, and we plant someone in the audience to bid it, we are basically stuck with the item if there's no higher bidder. It's unsold, we don't have our commission, and we have inventory. And because of the gentleman's rules we play by, we can't even let anyone know we haven't really sold the goods. It's registered as a sale at the price we've bid ourselves."

Wunnicke nodded thoughtfully. He saw the point at once.

"Now suppose, just suppose that we assign someone to record the highest legitimate bid, along with the identity of the bidder, just before we kick in to bid the reserve. Later, we call that guy, tell him that the winning bidder has defaulted, and if he's still interested, he can have the item at the last price he bid. Bingo! Happy client." Sarah searched Wunnicke's face for a reaction. He was too shrewd not to know that more was forthcoming.

"But what about the consignor who sets the reserve in the first place?" Wunnicke knew that she wanted him to ask, and he had enough respect for her to do so.

"We'll call him to explain that we didn't reach the reserve during the auction, but that we've got a buyer willing to pay just a bit less. My informal research shows that 90% of consignors will accept a bid close to the reserve when they realize that their alternative is an unsold item."

"Sounds like extra administrative work for us, Sarah."

There was a meaningful pause. Sarah leaned toward Wunnicke. "But the offer we make to the consignor can be less—sometimes considerably less—than the bid we have in hand." She leaned back, waiting.

"I see."

"And the profit would come right to us."

"Yes, I see." Wunnicke's excellent if narrow mind raced through the potential. It looked good *if*—and it was an enormous if—the transactions could be covert. The book-keeping, the paper work—that was easy enough. The risk would be in the people involved.

"Who would do the actual contacting?" Wunnicke crossed one leg, and began to touch his index fingers together.

"The interns and departmental assistants. None of them is here long enough to cause any trouble. They'd be flattered and thrilled to speak to clients and dealers, and probably wouldn't figure out the significance of the different prices, anyway."

Martin Wunnicke felt a prickle of heat at the back of his neck, along his thighs. The scheme was good, really good. She was something, this Sarah Dean.

49

Sarah ran the tip of her tongue over her lower lip. She had him; she knew it. And this was just the beginning.

"Can we put it into effect for six months, and I'll give you a figure analysis?" She spoke gently, insinuatingly.

"How'll you deal with the experts, the department heads?"

"Tell them privately, one by one. Nothing written down, of course. They're in their ivory towers, anyway. They'll do as they're told, especially if it's presented to them as nothing more than a business decision made primarily for the benefit of our clients."

Wunnicke loosened his tie, slid down in the chair, knees slightly parted. The discussion about the reserves had been an hors d'oeuvre; he was ready for the main course. His breathing quickened; he could feel his heartbeat against his starched white shirt.

Sarah knew what he wanted. The little game of thrust and parry was beginning in earnest. She drew out the thick book, bound in blue with gold engraving on the cover. "Here it is, Martin."

He moaned inadvertently, catching himself. She intoned softly, "The stock offering."

Chapter 7

Simon let himself in to his dark, silent apartment, and
headed for the small library, banging his shin on a
hassock. "Ouch. Damn," he muttered. He felt his way to his
favorite armchair, slumped into it, and breathed a heavy
sigh. "Lord. What a day." He sat in the dark, thinking over
the incredible events of the previous twelve hours, wondering whether or not the Cadwalader chair came with a curse.
That lunatic old man had a dignity about him. What was he
thinking? He believed in what he was doing, Simon had
concluded. He realized that he hadn't tackled anyone since
Pudgy Walters in prep school, and that he was a little sore
from taking down the "redcoat."

And that girl, that lovely young girl. I recognized her face
the moment I saw her. Oh, it can't be. He switched on the
lamp and went to the closet, where he rummaged until he
retrieved a small, unframed, dusty canvas. On it was a
portrait of a young nun, the first portrait he'd ever
attempted. It was a radiant countenance, lit from within by a
spiritual light. The portrait was signed "Simon Haden-Jones,
1967." Selena's face—well, almost, he told himself—stared at
him from the dusty surface. He hadn't misremembered.
Placing the canvas on the floor at a tilt where he could study
it, he poured himself a Scotch and returned to his chair.
Something was happening, something unbidden. It wasn't
just the girl, or the coincidence of her resembling the
painting, or even the strange incident with the intruder. It
was something inside him. He was being forced to look at
his life, and he wasn't sure he wanted to.

She's just so fresh, so eager. She makes me feel a bit...old. I haven't felt old before, he thought. He was dismayed by the notion, and tried to dismiss it—but it wouldn't go away.

"The persistence of memory," he muttered aloud, thinking of one of his favorite paintings by Salvador Dali. "So this is what he meant." His fatigue was great and he wanted to sleep, get drunk first if possible, but his mind wasn't going to allow it. It was after something, and he was to be its investigator whether he wished to or not.

He had been sixteen when he painted the portrait, and had just been sent away to prep school. His mind drifted back to that year. Something was slightly amiss at home. His mother had been distant and his father absent. He had been dispatched to boarding school, as were many of his friends, and his first year had been total misery. His sensitivity was a handicap, and when the rowdy, football-playing preppies found out that he *painted* for a hobby, they had been merciless. Thank God he was brilliant at tennis, which redeemed him, but only slightly, in their eyes. An Athenian in Sparta, he was lonely, angry, and felt a complete misfit.

Now in a mood for reminiscing, he went to the shelf that held his yearbooks and *Who's Whos*, pulled out the 1969 *Mischianza* of The Hotchkiss School, Lakeville, Connecticut, and turned to the page accorded to him as one of the graduating seniors. There he was: a thin, serious boy with unformed features and large ears. He read the inscription below the photograph:

HADEN-JONES, SIMON EDWARD (Haddie-Jay, Smasher, Ace), 1001 Fifth Avenue, New York, N.Y. 10021) First Tennis (3, 4 Captain 4); *The Review* (2, 3, 4); First Track (3, 4); Student Council (4); Glee Club (3); First Honor Roll (3, 4); *Insanity* (Co-founder); *Mischianza* (3, 4, Co-Editor); Current Events Club (2, 3, 4). "Risky"

52

Simon closed the book quietly and sat for a long time, remembering the unhappy years at an all-male prep school, and how he'd almost not made it through. Emotion washed over him in waves, and he let it come, abandoned himself to it. The memory of the terrible summer after his freshman year, when his world was shattered by his father's suicide, was still painfully raw. A long breath, like a sob, issued from him.

A great gulp of Scotch. He poured another. He thought of Yale, his "urban activism" when he'd taught art to ghetto kids at a New Haven housing project, the campus protests against the war in Vietnam, the long nights of studying and assuring each other that pot helped one's concentration. He searched the shelf for the Yale *Banner*, found it, and checked his picture: long sideburns, a straggling moustache. He couldn't suppress a rueful grin. *We thought we were going to change the world.*

Immersed in mental pictures of Yale, he drank. He'd lost his virginity in his sophomore year—it was the fashion—to a girl named Patty Eckhardt. It wasn't personal; it was just part of the whole "free love" ethic. It hadn't meant anything, and Simon had expunged the experience from his mind. Until now.

Another great gulp of Scotch. He filled the glass again.

Let's finish it, he thought—it's been a day for ghosts. He walked to a table where he opened a drawer and took out the scrapbook that Lavinia had started for him. It contained a half dozen or so newspaper clippings and several photographs. He carried it back to his chair, and opened it for the first time in years.

The first clipping was yellowing with age. In the margin someone had penciled the name of the newspaper and the date: *The New York Times*—December 12, 1979.

Lavinia Horace to wed
Simon Haden-Jones

Mr. & Mrs. George DeWitt Horace III, of Locust Valley, New York, announced the engagement of their daughter, Lavinia Paige, to Simon E. Haden-Jones, son of, Mrs. Samuel Higginson of St. Barthelmy, and the late Paul Haden-Jones. A June wedding is planned.

Miss Horace, known as Lally, is a special events coordinator at Tiffany & Co. She attended the Hewitt School and graduated from Miss Porter's and Franklin College in Lausanne, Switzerland. She was a member of the Junior Assembly, and was presented at the Thanksgiving Eve Ball of the New York Junior League, and the Debutante Cotillion and Christmas Ball. Her father is an investor and head of The Horace Fund. Her mother is the noted equestrienne.

Miss Horace is a great granddaughter of William Henry Horace, founder of the system of free libraries that bears his name, and former governor of the state of New York.

Mr. Haden-Jones is a painter and an assistant in the European Paintings Department at Endicottt's. He attended St. Bernard's School and Hotchkiss, and graduated cum laude from Yale University. His father, who retired as president of The First Bank of Delaware, was a painter and researcher of naval history.

His picture wasn't there, of course. Hers was. Done by Bachrach. She looked lovely, blonde and young. He turned the page of the scrapbook.

The next clipping was from *Antiques Weekly*, May 7, 1983.

Moving Up

Simon Haden-Jones, newly appointed head of the American Furniture department at Endicott's, expects a resurgence of interest in the finely crafted furniture of the Federal period. "I anticipate that demand will soar in this area, and that prices may increase as much as tenfold in the coming season," Mr. Haden-Jones predicts.

Haden-Jones was named to his new post following his acquisition for Endicott's of The Horace Collection, the first estate ever brought to auction in its entirety, including all contents of a fine Long Island home and the house itself, which is being marketed by Endicott's real estate division. Interest generated by the sale has helped to bring Endicott's out of a financial turndown, and has created excitement and record sales for the venerable auction house.

No photo. More Scotch. He turned the page. From the *New York Post*, February 14, 1984:

SOCIETY TOT
SLAUGHTERED
BY RUNAWAY CAB
PARK AVENUE PRAM DEATH TRAP

The infant son of Mr. & Mrs. Simon Haden-Jones, of 1160 Park Avenue, was killed today when a gypsy cab jumped the curb in front of the building and smashed the infant's baby carriage against the building's front wall. The baby's nanny, Ilsa Kagin, who arrived from Germany only two weeks ago, was unhurt but was treated for shock at the scene.

The twisted metal of the pram was hardly recognizable, according to police officer Jerry Fanelli, who was first to arrive on the scene. "It was a bloody mess," he said.

The child, George Edward Horace Haden-Jones, was pronounced dead-on-arrival at Lenox Hill Hospital. Cause of death was listed as internal injuries.

Officers at the scene described the taxi driver, Yamin Youssef, as a recent immigrant from Turkey who had been in the city for only two months. Police conducted a sobriety test on Youssef, but declined to comment on the results.

The Haden-Joneses are in seclusion tonight at an undisclosed location. He is the head of the American Furnishings Department at Endicott's Auction Gallery. Mrs. Haden-Jones is the former Lavinia Horace of Oyster Bay, great granddaughter of a former governor of New York.

The photo covered almost half of the page: a battered baby buggy, stupefied onlookers, a brick building with stains on the front. Simon stared at it and felt numb. Nothing.

A final clipping fluttered into his lap, the one he had added himself without bothering to paste it down. It was a middle paragraph from "Suzy's Column" in *The Daily News* for October 9, 1985:

It's official: The Simon
Haden-Joneses have called
it a day. Friends of Lavinia
Haden-Jones say she never
recovered from the tragic
death of their baby son last
year. But I keep hearing
stories about a certain
Lord somebody who turns
up at the exact spots where
Lavinia is watering while
Simon burns the midnight
oil at Endicott's. Hmmmm.

Simon flung the book aside. By now he was exhausted,
and wholly drunk. "Are you happy now?" he asked his
willful mind. "Are you happy?"

XOXOX

"What flair! What panache! I didn't know you had it in
you, old thing!"

Simon had been pulled from his somber reverie by the
jangling ringing of the telephone, something that happened
from time to time because he had yet to succumb to the lure
of the answering machine.

"Freddie, what are you babbling on about? Make sense."

"Don't tell me you haven't seen the late editions? Turn
on the news, old sport, right now! Channel 4!"

Simon reached for the remote control, and the set blazed
to life. Unfortunately, the story that had prompted Freddie's
call was over, and the weather announcer was pretending to
know something about meteorology. "Try the other
channels," suggested Freddie. "Perhaps one of them hasn't
run the story yet."

57

Success. When he switched to Channel 10, Simon heard the announcer say, "...has been identified as Henry Grenfell of East 19th Street, an unemployed actor originally from England. Mr. Grenfell's last role was as a British soldier in the film *Revolutionary*, and he evidently kept his costume. He is being held tonight at Bellevue Hospital for observation."

The picture showed Henry Grenfell, composed but with his powdered wig slightly askew, being shoved into a police car in front of Endicott's. His bearing was regal.

"Mr. Grenfell was in search of an antique chair, known as the Cadwalader, which is considered to be one of the most important surviving pieces of American Colonial furniture. It was recently consigned to Endicott's for auction. The would-be chairnapper said he was claiming the chair for King George III. We've heard of method acting, but this is going a little bit too far. The chair was unharmed, and the only casualty at Endicott's was a broken vase. Well, Mr. Grenfell was only a couple of centuries too late. Now for the weather."

Simon stared at the screen and muted the sound.

"It's simply brilliant, Simon, how did you think of it? You have deeply hidden talents!"

Simon was silent, uncomfortable.

"Don't tell me Alex Putnam dreamed this one up. He's too much of an ass for something this subtle."

"Freddie. Stop. This was no publicity stunt. That chap came out of nowhere and scared us to death. I had nothing to do with it."

"Feathers!"

"Really, Freddie."

"I think you've hit a lucky patch, Simon. Everything seems to be turning out well for you since you got hold of that blasted chair."

"I'm not so sure."

"Oh, come on! The publicity alone is worth millions. Wunnicke will of course attribute this to your genius. Let him!"

"But that old guy, Freddie. He...he was impressive, somehow. I guess he had passion."

Freddie choked back a smarmy retort.

"Don't worry your head about it, Simon. It's fantastic for Endicott's, and it's another coup for you."

"I'll speak to you about it tomorrow. All right?"

"Cheery bye, Simon; get some sleep."

XOXOX

Freddie put down the receiver and thought about sleep, knowing that tonight it wouldn't come. He hated these nights; they revolted him. But he knew.

He had tried everything: listening to the piano music of Debussy, studying the photographs of Atget, researching the fourteenth century for clues to its cultural remnants. But the urge was strong, like an inner clock that was nearing midnight. He may as well get ready.

He'd broken off completely with Roberto and his crowd. Showing up again at the loft, where heroin and cocaine were freely passed, and where men, dressed at every point in the gender spectrum, drifted in an out and were available for acts beyond his own imagination, would mean to him defeat and utter degradation.

He seemed to himself to be two different people in the same body. Tonight he would put on jeans and a shirt open to the waist, with various unusual amulets about his neck, and become once again Freddie Trosper—Freddie, whose hips swiveled when he walked, whom all the kids in Ottawa called "Frieda" when he was growing up. He had dealt with it then by using his brains and his humor. And that's how I deal with it now, he thought.

He looked into his Regency mirror, one of the exquisite appointments in his small but beautifully furnished Bank Street apartment, and saw Frieda. His hair, indeed his head, was unremarkable. Slightly balding in front, his Homburg obscured his wavy hair in his daytime life. Without the hat, he looked younger and more ordinary. He wondered whether anyone would look at him, whether he was anything to look at. Of one thing he felt certain: He wouldn't be easily recognized by anyone who knew him as Freddie Trowbridge of Bronte's.

He applied a dot of lip rouge, spreading it with the tip of his little finger, for that healthy glow. He tied a silk scarf around his neck. His last look around before leaving the apartment was an apologetic one: He apologized to his beautiful things because he was helplessly compelled to be ugly.

He walked out of the townhouse into the warm summer night, heading for Christopher Street, where he would be with his own kind, where he would blend into the pulsing crowd of his own kind. His steps quickened as he felt the electricity of the city night: lights, traffic, people, the muffled roar of an underground train, a hundred delights for the eyes. Shops in the Village were open at all hours. Freddie went into a pharmacy and bought a package of what they called in Ottawa "raunch raincoats," but that he had upgraded to *petites parapluies*. As he traversed the short blocks, he thought of what it must have been like in the 50s, when the Beats were there, living in cheerless cold water flats, writing or painting or making free love, determined to live and portray life in a new way, to shock and change society, forever outcasts and misfits. There was a purity in art then that didn't exist now.

Soho was a tarted-up version of what the Village once was. America wasn't rich in the '50s, except in ideas. The poverty of artists was quite real. The city's neighborhoods and establishments were rougher, meaner. What was it like for men of my persuasion? Freddie thought, and inwardly shuddered at the answer.

As he turned onto Christopher Street, he felt that atmosphere subtly change. There were gay couples, hand in hand, men's stores showing the newest Italian imports, sex shops, unmarked clubs. A low whistle came from a dark doorway, but Freddie walked on. He didn't want to look at anyone's face, or exchange biographies, or be involved.

"Hi, lover," a dark haired man in leather pants with studs, and wrist bracelets to match, stood right in front of him, pursing his lips in a grotesque parody of a kiss.

"Oh, my dear, I don't think so!" Freddie hurried on, walking west towards the Hudson River and the Trucks.

Although he knew how dangerous it was, particularly since the onset of the plague of AIDS, the Trucks had its attractions, the best being that it was always completely anonymous. Once inside, in the pitch black, he couldn't see anyone; and more important to Freddie, no one could see him. He'd never be recognized, and there would be no messy involvement. His breathing increased at the memory of the smell of them, the musky, indescribable odor of other men's bodies, their fluids.

He turned into the warehouse district at 11th Avenue, where there were no shops, no lights, no parade of strollers. He saw them in a row, like silver leviathans: huge semi trailers without their tractors, parked at loading docks where they seemed deserted. He climbed the stairs and approached the first one.

"Uh, uh, *uuhh!*" A groan, then a satisfied whimper.

A match flared in the back corner; he could make out five or six shadowy figures. He stepped in and a hand caressed his shoulder, pulling him into a rough embrace.

61

Chapter 8

"But darling, you *must* come! Anthony will understand!" Mona Elliott spoke into her French ceramic telephone as she surveyed herself in the smoked mirrors that lined the foyer of her Park Avenue duplex. Had she gained a pound or two, or was it the distortion of the mirrors? "I can't *believe* that the Princess is doing this to me, but Saturday night is the *only* time she'll be in New York, and she's *such* a dear." She cringed inwardly at the thought of even *being* in the city on a Saturday—nobody *ever* was, not even at the height of the season—let alone entertaining on a Saturday night, like a member of the bridge-and-tunnel set.

"Just a little supper for thirty...Jamie has agreed to cater, even on that ghastly night, and de Rochemont will do the flowers. Oh, and I thought I'd have a string trio playing soulful Russian music—you know, make her feel at home...hands across the sea and all that? Have you visited their hunting lodge near Petrograd? No? Wonderful. You will try to come? Oh, thanks, darling, and I owe you one."

Mona returned the telephone to its cradle and sighed. What a beastly thing to happen, and just as her social war with Judy Dunleigh was heating up to the temperature of molten lava. Judy was an arriviste, having crashed New York society on the arm of her Wall Street-tycoon husband; but she'd made all the right moves, given brilliant parties, and cozied up to the right decorators, writers and journalists. She'd even hired the right PR man, and was seen in the pages of *W*, the columns, and even *U'Omo Vogue*. Word was out that her apartment was being done for *Architectural*

Digest. She was a threat, the first one Mona had taken seriously in her twenty years of holding court for New York's rich, famous, and powerful.

Taking a small white jar from her dressing gown pocket, she peered closely at herself and then began to dab Retin-A on the skin near the hairline. The scars from the facelift were imperceptible, and with assiduous application of the cream, would soon fade into complete invisibility. There! She stood back and looked at herself, and liked what she saw. Connie (short for Cornelius), her husband of a quarter century, hinted darkly from time to time that she was getting both too thin and too rich, but she felt like a feather, and when she attended the Paris fashion shows, she could take the clothes right off the mannequins' backs. How many women of forty-five could say that?

She wandered into the living room and flicked on the chandeliers. A thousand slivers of light reflected softly on her priceless furniture, her soft Aubusson rugs. Was she getting tired of this look? Was it time to call Piero and start again from scratch? Something pagan and ruinous, perhaps, with broken columns and Roman busts? She'd call him right after the Princess' dinner. Shopping was such fun! And she could sell everything she had for a fortune at Endicott's without lifting a finger.

"Connie?" she called out as she heard the front door click open.

"No, it's me, Mrs. Elliott. Maria. I'm just going out tonight."

"Oh! Well, good night, but please use the servants' entrance next time."

"Yes, ma'am. But the back elevator isn't running."

"All right, Maria. Good night." The door closed quietly and she was alone in her glittering citadel.

Connie was coming home later and later these days, and

with Connie, Jr. grown and on his own, Mona was some-times lonely. Not that she spent much time at home—almost never! What with charity balls, committees, concerts, the house in the Hamptons for summer, she literally whirled from place to place. But often—was it becoming too often?—Connie called on man-about-town Mervyn Jepperson to escort her, claiming that his business was too pressing, or that he just couldn't face the "chitter-chatter." She under-stood. He was terrifically successful at running the family corporation (after the brief stint in the diplomatic corps when they were newlyweds), and he often said jocosely that he had to "keep her in diamonds."

Diamonds! As she looked up at the glittering chandeliers, she thought of her diamonds, her passion, her little loves. She could look at them now, the ones that weren't in the bank vault. Connie didn't like to come into her room when she had them spread out on the bed and was crooning to them, fondling them. But he wasn't home, and she could do as she liked. How strange to have a night at home! Too bad the duchess was gone; she had understood. But of course, now Mona had the duchess' leopard brooch and oodles of her rubies and emeralds. She loved John Bunch for helping her so much at the auction. He understood her, he really understood her.

"Charlemagne! Madame de Stael!" Two bichon frise pup-pies appeared at the door. "Want to see something pretty, my little darlings?" She swept them up, one on each arm, and walked down the long mirrored hall to her bedroom suite, thinking idly about the dinner for the princess—perhaps a balalaika player? the waiters and servants dressed in peasant costumes with boots?—when another idea entirely struck her. Sweeping the satin curtains aside, she fell across the bed, released the puppies, and picked up the telephone.

"Solange, darling. Mona. I have the most *wonderful* idea

65

for the cotillion next Fourth of July. We'll do a tableau of the American Revolution, and I'm going to buy the Cadwalader chair at Endicott's for Betsy Ross to *sit* on!"

)O(O(

Harris Tompkins sat back in his leather chair, loosened his tie, dropped his shoes, and began massaging his feet, never taking his eyes from the girl who stood with her back to him, mixing him a drink. It was fascinating, really fascinating: Whether her hair or her dress was the longer depended completely upon the angle of her movement. Sometimes they were exactly even, like, like...now. Sometimes the hair hung below, long, blonde and lustrous. She wore a bright blue suede minidress with intriguing cut-outs, matching high boots, and no jewelry—every middle-aged man's dream, the kind of girl that the suburban commuters glimpsed fleetingly, longingly, on MTV or rushing down a New York street. But she was beyond them, unattainable.

Harris sighed. He used to be that man, going home to the wife and kids in Connecticut, taking out the garbage, showing up at the suburban parents' groups and vapid social gatherings. Then the late night receptions and evening auctions started to take their toll on him. Jean, his wife, hadn't disagreed when he'd suggested getting an apartment for himself near Endicott's. It seemed a perfect solution. She didn't know about the churning and gnawing inside him, the discontent, the hunger. How could she? He had said nothing. Busy with the three kids, and caught up in the back-to-work, women-over-forty-as-executives mentality, she accepted things as they were. She didn't see the world he saw, the glittering, glamorous theatre where he, Harris Tompkins, was the star, the interlocutor, the consummate entertainer. They all loved him in a way Jean couldn't. And

66

he wanted to be named president of Endicott's American. Surely Wunnicke would do that much! You didn't become president by rushing home to the wife and kids in Southport. He knew that.

And the women! My God, the women! He turned his full attention back to the blonde in blue.

"Here you are, Mr. Tompkins. Now you must relax." She handed him a martini, sat on the ottoman, and began rubbing his feet. "You brave man!"

Harris swelled. He hadn't done much, just stayed firm and cool when a madman invaded his turf and interrupted his performance. He hadn't even made the news. But this nymphet, this New York Lolita who was in the audience with her manager, thought he was wonderful. And if she thought so, well, perhaps....

"I don't know how you do it," she purred. "Day after day, and all that traveling around the world, and the knowledge you have...you're just amazing." Her fingers were traveling up his trouser leg, gently stroking his calf. The signals were unmistakable. He felt the familiar flush of warmth around the groin, and wondered how to make it from this recumbent position to the bedroom without interrupting the mood, the flow, the electricity. Thank God he'd moved in completely three months ago; no more lying to Jean, no more guilt. He'd rediscovered, on 73rd street, the libidinous energy he hadn't felt since he was seventeen.

"Lily, sweetheart," he groaned as her fingers traveled up to his thigh, pulling at the fabric of his trousers. She leaned forward, her hair draping over his outstretched legs, and he saw the curvature of her buttock revealed by the dress. God! What flesh.

"Let's...get up." He kissed her lightly, but she was ahead of him, standing and holding out her hand. They walked to the bedroom, Harris touching her skin through the cut-outs

67

in the suede minidress. He turned her to face him, and embraced her hungrily, one hand cupping her rump, the other fumbling for her zipper under the cascade of hair. As he found it and began pulling it down, she nibbled his ear and whispered, "Mr. Tompkins, don't forget that you promised to introduce me to Paul McCartney."

Chapter 9

Selena let herself in to her apartment, closed the door and leaned heavily against it. The first involuntary movement was just a shiver, running from her head through her shoulders. It passed. Then she began to shake in earnest. Suddenly, her hand was no longer under her control. She dropped her purse, then her keys, and her trembling fingers were unable to thread the safety chain of the door, even when she used her other hand to steady them.

What's happening? she thought in alarm; what's happening to me? She was soon shaking so violently that she was afraid she couldn't make it to the pink futon, folded neatly against the far wall. She felt that if she let go of the door, the walls and floor would collapse, and she would be sent spinning out of control, into a black void, falling, clutching for a hand hold where there was none. Her chest tightened and she felt a flicker of pain. "Oh, no. Oh, no." She said it over and over. She held on to the doorknob as a drowning man clutches blindly at anything, anything that isn't water. After a long minute, the shaking lessened; the knot at her heart untied itself, and she was able to make her way, by halting steps, across the room.

"But it's over!" she kept telling her rebellious body. "It's all over." Unfolding the futon, she lay down on her back, looking at the ceiling and regaining her equilibrium. One lone crack in the otherwise pristine ceiling ran from overhead near her across the width of the room, and down to the header over the front door. She'd never noticed it before, and it seemed symbolic of something. A tear rolled down her cheek, then another, and soon she was crying with the greatest abandon she could ever remember. Breaking sobs wracked her slim body, and a humming sound issued from her throat. She lay, crying unreservedly, for many minutes, until there were no tears left. Only then was she able to think calmly about the traumatic events of the day.

She didn't know whether to thank or damn the rigid self-control that had enabled her to talk to the crazy man who had forced his way in to take the Cadwalader chair. She'd seen so many odd and unusual sights and people that morning that he seemed, at first, just another figure in an unfolding tapestry. Her father had always told her to "never panic or show fear if you are accosted—never," and she had learned her lesson well. Too well. Too well by half.

Suddenly, she felt anger. Why couldn't she have shrieked and frozen like the assistant, ceding control of the situation to someone else? Why did she have to be strong? She wanted to be weak and silly. She wanted to be with Neal, bashing around Europe having fun, being carefree. Other girls her age took their pleasures. They didn't worry terribly about their careers, or work when they didn't have to. For the first time, she felt that there might be something wrong with her, wrong with her upbringing, wrong with her choices.

She sniffled, and ran a hand through her hair. She needed a cup of tea. Mother always made a cup of tea when she felt ruffled, which was almost never.

Selena got up slowly, retrieved her keys and purse from where they'd fallen, and put them on top of the bookcase made of green plastic dairy cubes artfully stacked. In the tiny galley-style kitchen, she put on the kettle and rummaged for the tea and strainer. Stiff and black, the tea would steady her; it always had.

It was almost four in the afternoon when she finished her tea and regained her perspective. Things happened, that was all, and one didn't alter or question one's life because of random occurrences, such as the intruder at Endicott's.

And one only cried like she had over things that had been waiting to be cried over for a long time. She knew what it all was: the break-up with Neal; the maddening imprecision of their status; the move to New York City, with its terrible anxieties; the feeling that she couldn't ever go back after this summer—though back to *what* wasn't really clear; the lessening of her family life, an inevitability. It was all of that.

It had all come so fast, and so relentlessly. This afternoon had merely been the occasion to break down. The reasons were many. Mr. Haden-Jones had suggested that she go home as soon as the incident with the intruder was over and he had been led safely away by Endicott's security men, but she had stayed, wanting to be present at the interns' orientation meeting. She wanted her employee card, wanted to meet the other interns and to hear about the curriculum in store for them. As it happened, she was already a celebrity. Mr. Putnam, the public relations director (she recognized him as the blonde man from the elevator), introduced her and talked about how to handle crisis publicity and damage control with the media. (Two girls scribbled furious notes. Selena surmised that they were in the press department.) The interns were an interesting lot.

She thought back to the incident. Mr. Haden-Jones had been simply, well, wonderful. If the situation had not been so serious, she would have laughed aloud to see him tip-toeing up behind the costumed man, then flying through the air with his hair on end and a look of rank determination on his face. His tackle had been masterful: The man, who went over with an "oof," landed in the corridor and thus damaged nothing. When his old gun clattered to the floor, Selena simply picked it up and put it aside, surprised by its weight. Mr. Haden-Jones, bow tie

71

askew, sat on the intruder's back, and said to Arabella, "Get security—quickly." He and Selena simply looked at each other until Arabella came back with six security guards yelling wildly. Then he smiled at her wanly, hitched up a fallen suspender, and said, "Good job, Miss...er...Fraccese?"

She walked to her window and again took in the cityscape: the brownstones, the hurrying people, the traffic coursing through the streets. Today had been an urban baptism, that was all. Now she was a New Yorker.

"Terwilliger!" She uttered the first nonsensical expletive she had adopted on coming to Wesleyan, and bolted to the sink, depositing the cup and saucer. She had promised her father that she would call before it was too late in Florence. Already it was 10:30 p.m. at Villa Fraccese. If she called, he probably would be reading. She touch-dialed the overseas code frantically, then abruptly jabbed at the phone, breaking the connection. What will I tell him about today? she wondered, knowing that he must not feel that she was in danger. He was concerned about her, but expected her to handle whatever situation life might present. Was this the one that was too frightening? Would this revelation cause him to insist that she move in with some of their friends, where she could be properly chaperoned (and stifled)?

Could she carry it off? Could she call him and speak calmly about the turbulent emotions she'd just endured, the incredible experiences of the last eight hours? She'd have to speak to him calmly if she wanted things to stay as they were. A wistful sadness settled on her as she sat down and placed her call.

"*Pronto.*"

"Papa...."

"*Signorina Fraccese. Como le va? Va bene?*"

"In English, Papa. I'm a New Yorker now."

"Oh, a New Yorker, *cara* Selena? All right. And how was

your first day at the big auction house?"

"Very...exciting, Papa."

She realized then that she would tell him nothing, and hoped that he would never know. After hearing from him about the gardens at home, her mother's current trip to England to visit her aunt Blanche, and her father's pending journey to negotiate with the minister of culture in Moscow, Selena felt, reluctantly, that she should say good-bye. Her father always made her feel like a beloved little girl, safe and warm. It had been a tonic to speak to him; she had needed it. But more talking was dangerous. Her own fear might slip out, and he was perceptive. After assuring him that she had enough money, and that she would ring up and call on the Italian ambassador and his wife, she said a fond farewell.

"*Arrivederci*, Papa."

"In English, please. Good-bye, my lovely Selena."

A click. The call ended. A little shiver ran over her and an odd feeling that she soon recognized as guilt played about her. She'd felt it only once before, when she had concealed the existence of Neal from him. Her original plans for the summer had been conveyed as a trip with "a friend" whom she would bring to Florence in August.

She shook her head, hard. *No, I will not think about Neal, not now!* Because...because...I'm lonely. And...I'm hungry.

She took out the New York telephone directory and ran her finger down the columns of incredibly tiny print. She touched the number.

"Shecky's Pizza—it ain't matzo—hang on." The shout was so loud she winced, and felt that passers-by must have heard it on the street. After perhaps a minute, the voice came back, shouting, "What'll it be?"

"Is Julio there?"

"Hang on." Another minute's wait.

"Julio Martinez here."

73

"Hello, Julio, it's Selena Fraccese."

"Who?" The din grew louder, joined with a siren wailing in the background.

"Selena Fraccese—the girl with the futon?"

"Oh, hi, Miss Selena of Endicott's. I thought you might be my agent. What can I do for you?"

"Well, Julio, I'd love a pizza. Do you deliver?"

"Sure, I'll bring it over myself. Let's see…83rd and First, isn't it? Only…(his voice sunk to a theatrical whisper) I have one terrible problem."

"What is it, Julio?"

"I don't know what you want on your pizza!" He laughed a rich, merry laugh, and Selena joined in.

Chapter 10

"**M**r. Haden-Jones—this is Hadley Brown speaking." The clipped, imperious voice on the phone made Simon bridle with distaste. It wasn't merely that he and Hadley Brown were business rivals, seeking the same rare treasures, knowing and pursuing the same collectors from the same families. He simply didn't like the man.

"Yes, Mr. Brown. What can I do for you?"

It was three days after the incident backstage at Endicott's, and things in the American Furniture department had settled into the quiet and orderly routine of preparing for the major fall auctions, and running the smaller summer ones. Simon didn't welcome the intrusion of Hadley Brown.

"It's about the chair, Mr. Haden-Jones. The Cadwalader."

"Yes?" Simon was damned if he would be polite, much less forthcoming.

"I have a serious buyer for the piece...."

Simon interrupted him. "Then we'll be pleased to see your client at the auction on September fifth."

"I'm afraid you don't understand, Mr. Haden-Jones."

Simon's annoyance was growing. He didn't like Hadley Brown's voice any more than he did the man, and he considered simply saying a curt good-bye and cutting him off by hanging up. Not done. He must hear him out. "Yes?"

"Since the unfortunate incident involving the chair last Monday, the Peabody family has decided that it really isn't safe with you, and they wish to withdraw it from sale."

Simon was stunned. The sheer effrontery of the call was beyond his understanding. There had been a contest between him and Hadley Brown, and he had won. It was over. Didn't the man ever give up?

"We have a signed contract, Mr. Brown, and as we've demonstrated, the chair is quite safe with us. Good day."

But the dealer continued: "The Peabodys wish to rescind the contract, Mr. Haden-Jones. Their attorneys are at work on it right now."

My God. Could they? Simon always had conducted business as a gentleman. He never perused contracts for their legal loopholes. Until Wunnicke took over, a handshake and a verbal agreement had often been enough to consign a work of art for auction at Endicott's, and the trust between the owner and the expert had been the seal. Things were changed, unutterably changed.

"I am unable to speak with you further about this matter, Mr. Brown. Thank you for your call." Simon hung up abruptly. He knew and respected the Peabodys, and he would never threaten them with legal reprisals. A call from an Endicott's attorney might well fling them further into Hadley Brown's embrace.

"Arabella! Get me Grace Peabody on the phone, quickly— Philadelphia!" Simon rummaged frantically through his desk, gathering material. "And ring Alex Putnam. I need all the press clippings and transcripts to date about the Cadwalader chair, and an outline of all the pre-sale publicity he's planned. Oh, and get Delbert; ask if he has a draft of the catalogue copy, and the *Forthcomings* article. Now, please."

Arabella appeared at the door, astounded by all the overlapping requests, unable to sort them out. She looked at Simon with a helpless gaze and lifted her hands.

"In that order, Arabella. Get Miss...get Selena to help you. Now move!"

The girl's eyes widened, and she disappeared from the doorway, only to reappear moments later. "Mrs. Peabody is

76

not at home, Mr. Haden-Jones. The butler said so."

"Is she out of town?"

"I didn't ask."

"Well, call back and *ask*, Arabella! And find out when I can reach her. This is important."

"Yes, sir."

Simon ran his fingers through his smooth, dark hair. Think, think, he flagged himself. The garage. Yes. He jabbed at the phone.

"Century Garage."

"This is Mr. Haden-Jones. Can you uncover my car, gas it, and have it ready in half an hour?"

"Is that the old Merc with the tarp, sir? Let me check." An interminable hold. "Yes, sir—she starts right up."

"Thank you. I'll be around."

Simon waited impatiently for Arabella to reappear, drumming his fingers on the desk, stabbing at his blotter with his pen. Unable to sit still, he jumped up and strode toward the door, nearly colliding with the harried girl as she entered.

"She's in town, Mr. Haden-Jones. Mrs. Peabody. I mean, she's not away."

"Good, good, great, thank you!" Simon grabbed the phone and touched Freddie's number.

"French furniture," a nasal voice intoned, complete with the requisite French accent.

"Is Mr. Trowbridge in? This is Mr. Haden-Jones calling."

"Freddie's on the floor doing an auction until four. May I have a message?"

"Yes. Please tell him he was right, and that there's thunder in the glen. I'll call him tomorrow and explain."

"Thunder in the glen?" The voice was puzzled.

"He'll understand."

Simon took a leather portfolio from behind a cabinet and began packing it. This time it was Selena who appeared at

77

the door. He blushed and averted his gaze.

"Here are the publicity releases and clippings for the Cadwalader chair, Mr. Haden-Jones. Is there something wrong?"

"A small problem, Selena." He was mumbling again. He willed himself to look her in the eyes. "I have to go to Philadelphia to see the owners right away."

"May I get you anything else?"

This girl seemed to penetrate his skin and go directly to a tender place where only one living creature had ever touched him before—his son, George Edward, that smiling, happy baby boy.

"No, no—I mean, yes. Please ask Arabella about the copy for the catalogue and *Forthcomings.*

"She's gone for them right now."

"Well, that's fine, fine."

He noticed her slight smile, the way her hair moved as she turned in the doorway, the beauty of her fleeting profile. Suddenly, that vision was replaced by the face of Arabella, who was wheezing and panting. She handed him a stack of shiny proof sheets. "They're not corrected yet, but the layout's final."

He looked appreciatively at the sheets, marveling at the beauty and richness of Endicott's private publications.

"Thanks, Arabella. I'll be back tomorrow. Please defer all major crises, and handle the small ones yourself."

She gulped and tried to look her competent best, tugging at the hem of her blouse, which had come untucked.

Simon stuffed the papers into a leather portfolio, grabbed his raincoat, and dashed down the hall, brow furrowed and lost in thought. He pushed through the security door, and was unaware of the individual people in the reception area, aware only that they were there in a gaggle. The full bustle of the day was upon this great marketplace of art.

The elevator opened, and in his haste he nearly collided

with a befuddled man carrying a marble bust. (Victorian—probably an interpretation from classical sources of Minerva or some other goddess, highly sentimentalized, he thought in the split second his eyes passed over the bust.)

The man asked rather huffily for appraisals.

"What? Oh, oh—third floor. Just stay on." He pushed the button for three, then for one. The man eyed him warily, thinking perhaps that he might be a murderer—maybe the murderer of Granny's cherished bust. He crushed the bust to his chest, and lost no time exiting the elevator at three.

Once on the street, Simon broke into a lengthy stride that carried him quickly the few blocks to the garage. He descended the cement ramp, and spied the dull green patina of the 1967 Mercedes-Benz. A convertible. Aunt Georgina had quite amused herself, both in buying the car in what she called her "middle-aged fling," and in leaving it to Simon, an adored nephew. Simon had cherished the Mercedes, and couldn't imagine driving anything else.

He nodded to the attendant, and flung his materials and raincoat into the back seat. Slipping into the leather of the driver's seat, he looked at the tortoise shell inlay, and took sensual pleasure in the feel of the ivory-handled gearshift. Too bad the day was overcast, and the air pregnant with rain. Probably there would be no chance to drive on the highway with the top down, and enjoy the glorious rush of air and sense of freedom it gave him.

Pulling into traffic, he maneuvered downtown toward the Holland Tunnel, marveling at the abbreviations called neighborhoods. Many seemed to extend only one or two blocks before they were supplanted by something completely different in character: here, elegant apartment houses with their doormen; there, renovated tenements with storefronts on the first floor; now, sleek office buildings with computer-designed plazas. Then the business blocks, tall glass towers punctuated by old brownstones which had survived, and which now housed private libraries, foundations, foreign churches, university alumni associations. He registered the panorama, but his mind was still racing. The chair. He had to keep the chair.

The Mercedes moved into the wholesale merchandise neighborhoods, first with showcase windows on the street, then the unpretentious areas where the manufacturing, sewing, and work got done. Down Broadway to Astor Place, past throngs of students and the campus attendants, record shops, restaurants, pizzerias, discos, funky clothiers; through arty Soho to lower Manhattan, where life got rougher, drearier; beyond Little Italy and Chinatown.

With a start, Simon realized how seldom he went out into this variegated world. His job, the precious world of the Upper East Side, his ring of acquaintances was growing smaller and smaller, until he felt encased in a little ornamental bubble: a miniature man in a Faberge egg. He made himself a promise to go to Chinatown for dim sum as soon as he got back, with...Freddie? Maybe he could take Arabella and Selena for a "thank you for taking over" excursion. He flushed. Simon, old man, don't lie to yourself, he thought. You wouldn't take Arabella to the corner deli. Why use her as camouflage?

The answer to this question kept pushing insistently into his consciousness: Because I'm too old for Selena! I'm too tired, too emotionally spent, and dammit, I'm in love with her and it doesn't suit me just now. There. He had thought it, said it to himself. He felt better somehow, and drove the wonderful old car past the downtown government buildings toward the tunnel.

No traffic at this time of day; good. Soon the New Jersey Turnpike was under his wheels, and he began to relax as the car hummed along. The sky turned a sulfurous pewter. The smokestacks belched forth plumes of chemicals, and he thought of Carl Sandburg and Edward Hopper and Upton Sinclair and all their warnings about the horrors of industrial America, long before radioactive pollutants and contamination. Simon's life had always been aloof from all that, but he knew it was there, lurking, just as he was aware that his privilege extended only to the very few.

It began to rain, first one splash on the windshield, then two, then a spattering. He turned on the windshield wipers, listening to their rhythmic back-and-forth, and suddenly had a sense of memory so powerful that he nearly let go of the wheel. He was five years old, standing in the back seat of another Mercedes, and Aunt Georgina was at the wheel, singing a risqué French song as they motored down a country highway in the rain. He had caught her eyes in the rear view mirror. She laughed, reached back to ruffle his hair, and asked if he heard the windshield wipers singing. Perplexed, he had asked, "Singing? Singing what?"

"They're singing 'sigh-munn, sigh-munn, sigh-munn'— don't you hear?" He had nodded happily. "They'll always sing 'sigh-munn' for you, darling." He wondered if they sang "sigh-munn" for him today.

"Blast it, anyway." He dropped his change as he neared a toll. "I don't have time to daydream. What's the matter with me? I must plan what I'm going to say to Grace Peabody." But he didn't.

)0(0(0(

"God *damn* Haden-Jones!" Alex Putnam slammed the door to his sanctum. His assistant, Diana, sat unruffled in the Jacobean chair, this week's treasure for Alex's den. She knew a tirade was coming. "I hate that upper-class prick! He causes me more trouble than anyone in this whole damn company. London has heard about his little drama, and I'm getting the heat for being crass."

"But it really wasn't his fault...." Diana was cut off by a furious glare. Alex, who was from the privileged upper-middle class, evidently couldn't help hating those who had been born with a slightly larger silver spoon in their mouths.

"Do we *know* that? Do we know that Haden-Jones didn't hire the crackpot with the musket himself just to get his name in the papers *once again*? Well, I fooled him. He wasn't mentioned *one time* in the media." Alex put his fingers through his suspenders and smirked. "Not *one time*. I'm not here to be Simon's personal press agent."

"Alex, really." She was having trouble hiding her disgust.

"Did you know that Wunnicke called me to ask why Haden-Jones wasn't mentioned or interviewed? Wunnicke himself? He wants his fair-haired boy to be Endicott's mascot. Well, I still have something to say about the news that comes out of this press office."

"Alex, lower your voice or you'll scare the interns. They're staying late to impress you."

"Yeah, yeah, yeah. Well, we'll take care of simple Simon once that damn chair of his is out of here."

"You're being bitchy, Alex. It's just part of our job, and he's really making it easier for us."

"*Easier?*" Alex was heating up again, and Diana saw that there was no winning him over.

"Has it occurred to you that Wunnicke might be thinking of making him president?" She asked it quietly.

Alex reeled as if he had been shot. Diana hurried on. "Look, I'm meeting *Connoisseur* for drinks. Want to join us?"

"No, thanks, not in the mood. Sell them on doing a pretty story about the Stanislas Collection, will you?"

"I'll try my best. Good night." Diana slipped out of the office. It must be love, she thought.

Chapter 11

"Thunder in the glen?" Freddie blinked, looked again at the note, then roared with laughter. "Oh, Simon, I love you, *mon ami*, but you're such a stiff! Thunder in the glen." He shook his head, gathered his papers, adjusted his silk ascot, and headed off for the Oak Bar at the Plaza. The afternoon sale had gone well, and he enjoyed conducting them when Christian was away. A born showman, he could cajole and humor the audience into bidding just a little more than they wanted to bid. He made them laugh, which was why he was assigned only the smaller auctions at Bronte's. The major sales were deadly serious and carried out with the decorum of a royal coronation—which was decidedly not Freddie Trowbridge's style.

He laughed under his breath as he strolled up Fifth Avenue on his way to meet a French art dealer, stopping to check his reflection in the shop windows, adjusting the Homburg and his ascot. Although he loved his hat, summer could be brutal. Thank God he moved, generally, from one air-conditioned space to another, and usually by taxi, which minimized his discomfort. June in New York was one of his favorite times.

As he walked on, drawing some interested stares, he thought about Simon's message. What could it mean? Some problem with the chair? Probable. Politics at the auction house? Usual. Girl trouble? Not likely at this point: Simon seemed to be pouring all his prodigious energies into his career. Since his marriage ended, he seemed determined to be the best in the business—the most knowledgeable scholar, the most respected department head, the most valuable procurer of treasures for Endicott's, which he revered with an almost childish fervor. Freddie had decided that this was a rechanneling of the competitive spirit Simon had developed at tennis. Freddie knew that Simon took every opportunity to play, and that he was deadly serious about winning. Simon also spent every available Sunday afternoon watching professional football, carefully studying the game's strategies. To Freddie, this was incomprehensible. Idiotic male rites. Then he admitted that his own sub-rosa life would be just as incomprehensible to Simon. What they both shared was a great passion for excellence of concept and beautiful things, and a scholarly and inquisitive bent of mind.

But there was something stronger that held them in their improbable friendship. They both had been deeply hurt. Their paths, so disparate, had crossed, and each recognized the wound in the other, without ever voicing it, or even discussing the painful events of their individual pasts. It was a kind of fellowship-of-two in the brittle, elegant and competitive world they inhabited.

Freddie's mind went back to the genesis of the code phrase "thunder in the glen." While taking a tour of the Metropolitan Museum as young interns, they both had been struck by the technique of Cézanne, and had been deep in conversation about the uses of the palette knife in impressionism when they were suddenly aware that the assistant director of the museum was staring at them coolly. All eyes were on them.

"Gentlemen, this is an instructional tour, not a social hour."

Titters. Simon reddened, Freddie grinned idiotically.

"May I suggest that you take your conversation down to the cafeteria while the rest of us learn?"

The class walked on and left the two of them on a bench

in the cool grey gallery. They were both embarrassed and humiliated. They stared straight ahead at a huge landscape painting of Bierstadt's on the opposing wall showing a storm forming over rolling hills in the Hudson River Valley.

"Thunder in the glen," Simon muttered with the force of an expletive. Freddie broke into a nervous giggle. Suddenly, they were both laughing hysterically, the release of tension. "Thunder in the glen" became their code phrase for trouble. Luckily, neither of them had had occasion to use it in years.

Freddie, unaware of the mental odyssey that was taking Simon into his past these days, thought: What made him think of that now?

His stroll was ending. He turned onto 59th street and tripped up the steps to the venerable Plaza. He loved the hotel; it seemed to him the essence of all the glamour and romance of New York. In the Plaza's fountain, Zelda Fitzgerald had cavorted in the 1920s. Heads of state, stars and celebrities had stayed there. Horse drawn carriages, standing in front, ready to take passengers on leisurely rides through Central Park, awaited their evening fares. Freddie went through the doors, and heard the light harmonies of the string trio playing in the opulent Palm Court.

He was meeting Olivier de Palance, a French dealer in from Paris, who had clients both wishing to sell and wishing to buy. Freddie was interested in all the consignments he could find from Europe: auction fever was at a frenzied pitch, and the prices achieved at Bronte's and Endicott's were absurdly high. Olivier had been an invaluable connection.

In the Oak Bar, Olivier sat at a table in the corner, overlooking Central Park South.

"*Bonjour*, Freddie, *ça va?*" He smiled pleasantly as he motioned Freddie to a seat.

"*Bienvenue*, Olivier. I see you're out of the old gate ahead

85

of me."

"*Comment?*"

"You already have your drink, *ami*."

"Oh! *Oui, oui, bien sur.* Please" Olivier held up an elegant arm, and waved a gold cigarette case at the waiter. He was expensively dressed in an Armani suit and Italian silk tie.

Freddie ordered a vermouth cassis, and settled into the gentlemanly dark leather chair.

"Tell me about Drouot's Paris auctions. Are they fetching the same prices we are here?"

"Yes, but not so outrageous for the money. But the highest prices ever for the finest things."

Freddie understood that, just as international political and financial events seemed to come in waves that transcended the boundaries between nations, so did trends in the art world. There was simply no doubt that the Japanese, circling the globe with fortunes gained in the electronics and automotive industries, were driving the trend.

The men soon fell into a business discussion of who had what collections, who had fallen on hard times, who had made fortunes. Some of them were made dishonestly, through drug importing or insider trading, but they were fortunes, nonetheless. Freddie knew that these people would buy all the fine old antiques they could get, purchasing a past that they never possessed. He sighed. They were his best customers, just as the fine old families with inherited collections were the ones who would sell. Often they had to. It made him sad, somehow, this tyranny of money.

After the business talk became friendly banter, Olivier said, "Let's have dinner in my suite tonight."

Startled, Freddie asked "Why?" He knew that Olivier was homosexual, but there had never been *that* between them.

"I have a little entertainment arranged for us."

Freddie agreed, curious but not a little discomfited. He

had always been exquisitely careful to keep his private pleasures far from his work, although there were many in the business who quite openly engaged in liaisons. He felt that that would be disastrous for him, without connections and without family.

The two natty men entered the deep, wood-paneled elevators, and went directly to the tenth floor. Olivier's suite was a study in faded grandeur: reproduction Louis XVI chairs, tasseled curtains, moiré walls, all just a little tired, a little dated. Freddie was surprised to see a large buffet table laid.

"I've invited a few friends." Olivier smiled at Freddie, proffering a canapé. "Have some caviar, *mon ami.*"

Freddie took the canapé. It was delicious. Beluga, no doubt about it.

The doorbell rang, and two young men entered. Freddie recognized one as a specialist in Russian enamels from A La Vielle Russie, just across the plaza. The other was introduced as Lamborg Whittaker, with no elaboration. Freddie smiled amiably, and made small talk about films and novels. Soon, two more young men arrived, individually, and were introduced as Carter and Wilhelm. Olivier suggested that they begin, and waiters brought in and set up steaming chafing dishes.

Freddie's curiosity grew as he consumed the *blanquette de veau* and washed it down with crisp white Chardonnay. Olivier was certainly up to something, and it was decidedly not business. After coffee and petits fours, uniformed busboys whisked away the tables with the remnants of the feast, and Olivier rose with his glass. "Gentlemen, please move your chairs back along the walls."

There was general scraping and murmuring. Lamborg said, "Whoopee," for no apparent reason.

"Gentlemen—*je vous presente—Les Ballets Copacabana!*"

With a clap of his hand, the door to the second room of

the suite opened, music swelled, and a corps de ballet flitted gracefully into the center of the room to the strains of *Swan Lake*. Beautifully costumed, the dancers began the slow adagio. It took a moment for the surprised guests to realize that what they were seeing were not ballerinas, but young men, boys, really. Their perukes and make-up enhanced the illusion. As they twirled and performed arabesques, Freddie noted that they wore no tights, only the tiniest G-strings under their tulle skirts. The exaggeration was slight and artistic, so rather than looking like college boys in drag, the young dancers nearly carried off the impersonation. Their dancing was exquisite.

Olivier smiled with delight. The entertainment was obviously exactly right for his audience. After the beautifully performed *Swan Lake*, the boys lined up for a rowdy Can-Can, to the strains of *Gaite Parisienne*. The formality of the ballet was flung aside, and the dancers camped, flirted, and blew kisses. There was general good humor and laughter. Only the man identified as Wilhelm watched intently with steely, glittering eyes. At the climax of the dance, each boy threw himself into the lap of one of the onlookers. Freddie found himself enveloped in a sea of white tulle, which nearly knocked off his hat.

"My place or yours? Or here?" the young man asked.

XOXOX

Hours later, when he arose and touched the soft, curling hair of the young man who slept so quietly in his bed, and smelled the fresh, sweet smell of him, Freddie felt sick with tenderness and need. All his wit, artifice, and detachment left him. He had crossed some invisible line, he knew that— but he didn't yet know what it was.

Chapter 12

Simon found a parking space near Society Hill. The drive had been a long one, and he was weary, but the urgency he had felt that morning was still with him. He had tried again and again to imagine meeting with Grace Peabody, to work it out in his mind, but other pictures kept interrupting. He thought of Theodora van Plant, the most serious affair he'd had after his marriage ended. Theodora! What great long legs, and a mane of hair like a palomino, and a laugh that tinkled like crystal chimes. He'd needed the fun, the activity, the midnight picnics with the Mercedes, the dancing all night at Nell's, the sex. But when she began to talk seriously, the ache in him returned, and he couldn't go on. He felt hollow, empty, and though he adored her, he concluded that he didn't love her. At least, not enough.

"You'll be sorry, Simon darling," she had whispered. And he was. Six months after Simon failed to propose, someone else did. Ah, Theodora.

Up the steps to the beautiful brick townhouse. Simon took a deep breath and lifted the heavy bronze knocker. Three clangorous thuds reverberated within. Simon heard measured steps coming toward the door, which swung open soundlessly on large brass hinges.

"Sir?" McManus, the butler, was attired in a black suit with white gloves.

"Is Mrs. Peabody at home?" It occurred to him that, with his large black portfolio, he might appear to be a door-to-door salesman.

"Is she expecting you, sir?"

"It's Simon Haden-Jones—er, tell her it's Camilla's son, Simon."

"Please wait, sir." The butler motioned Simon into the entrance hall and went away with his measured steps. The hall was narrow, but had a stately air about it. Grandeur could be implied as well as stated, and that was the case in many of the gracious old town houses of the eastern cities. Simon sat, fidgeting, wondering why he'd come, and what the devil he was going to say. What if Grace Peabody wouldn't see him? He was counting very much on her good manners.

"Simon, dear."

He looked up and saw her, a slim, imperial figure with a lacquered helmet of blonde hair, descending the stairs, her hand outstretched.

"How nice of you to stop in. And just in time for tea. We're upstairs in the library. Won't you join us?"

Simon took her hand and squelched the impulse to kiss it, or to go down on one knee. As a little boy, he'd thought of her as Queen Grace, and himself as a knight in her noble service, roaming her dominions on a stick horse.

"And how is Camilla? She so rarely comes up from the Caribbean."

So this is how she'll play it, he thought, bemused. Unless I force the issue, she'll never even mention the chair. He decided to temporize, watch for openings, go along. Just a social call. Just Simon dropping in for afternoon tea, and a little unexpected, but completely manageable. He ran his fingers through his hair, and shook his head to clear it. As they ascended the stairs, she spoke cordially of mutual friends, marriages, the weather. They moved, footsteps muffled by a thick grey carpet. Simon remembered the wood-paneled bath, and asked if he might freshen up. She nodded—"of course"—and said to come on to the third door

90

on the right when he was ready. He closed the door quietly and turned on the tap, splashing cold water on his face. He straightened his tie and ran a comb through his hair. Hazarding a smile, which was slightly lopsided, but which would see him through, he washed his hands in the dull white marble lavabo, and took three deep breaths.

"Ah, there you are." He entered the richly paneled room with its carved wainscoting and recessed bookcases of the darkest mahogany. A Queen Anne table, laden with silver pots, small china plates, delicate sandwiches and cakes, and lemon slices sat before the fireplace. The Cadwalader chair had been in this room when he first saw it.

"Sit there, Simon, and put your...your case by the door. There. Lemon or milk?"

He hated tea. "Neither, thanks." But he helped himself liberally to the sandwiches.

A cousin was in the room with them, Vanessa Wood-bridge or something, a rather sour, unmarried woman who had made some success as an amateur anthropologist. Simon had met her before in passing. She alone seemed alert to the potential of his being there unannounced. Grace Peabody's iron charm was unchanged and unchanging.

"Have you had a good season at Endicott's?" Grace asked pleasantly, pouring tea. The owlish Vanessa looked at him with anticipation.

"Yes, thank you, Grace. Sales are quite wonderful."

"Yes, I've heard. Mr....Wunnicke? Seems very...forward-looking. But he's a little...boisterous for our taste."

Simon read the subtext of her "boisterous": crude, pushy, nouveau riche, crass, and...Midwestern. "He's not one of us, though, is he?" She smiled regally.

One of us.

One of us. No, he's not one of us. "He's from Kansas, I believe. Phenomenally successful there."

91

The three fell into silence. Simon munched his sandwich, thinking of the time, thinking of tomorrow, the rush of his life, and getting back to his office, his work, Selena. Time seemed almost suspended in this house. It moved in a decorous, slow minuet. Or was his life suddenly going too fast? He wasn't sure, but the seduction of repetitive rituals and good manners was not to be given into today. "Grace, I need to speak to you about the Cadwalader chair."

There was an awful silence, as if he'd committed some unpardonable faux pas, yelled obscenities at a funeral, run naked through church. The afternoon light played across the paneling, the silver. A clock ticked. Grace sipped her tea.

"I see," she said icily. "Vanessa, will you excuse us, please?"

Deprived of her fun, Miss Woodbridge got up with resignation, and moved sullenly toward the door, flashing an irritated glance at her cousin.

"Thank you, dear. Please close the door behind you." An unmistakable slam. "Yes, Simon?" Grace let him know how painful she found this breach of etiquette.

"Grace, I had a call from Hadley Brown. He said you're going to withdraw the chair from Endicott's. Is this true?"

"Simon, I had hoped to do this quietly, but I suppose nothing is ever quiet at Endicott's any more."

"But why, Grace? We're doing our utmost to do a beautiful presentation for you, and to find a buyer worthy of your chair's provenance. Why, we're reaching every corner of the world with our publicity and our publications. Let me show you what we've done." Simon leaped up and strode toward his leather portfolio.

"That's not necessary, Simon. I don't question your work."

"Then why, Grace? Why?"

She summoned her powers and arrayed them, speaking with measured care. "Simon, you know how painful it is for

92

us to part with the chair. What we most hoped for in entrusting it to your care was discretion."

"But...." Simon leaned forward, and she silenced him with two fingers.

"No matter how...tasteful...your presentation may have been, we...I...find the results of that presentation scandalous. You know how we feel about any kind of publicity, and when Cartwright heard about a lunatic actually getting into Endicott's and attacking the chair, it was the last straw."

"Let me explain...." Once again, she silenced him.

"We feel that the Cadwalader is being exploited, Simon. It hurts and embarrasses our family. Now don't protest! I know you too well to think that you don't understand."

Simon was growing increasingly miserable with each word she spoke. The pain of it was that he did understand. How mercantile the merchandising of her fine antique must seem to her, how vulgar. She, who had lived with the chair, sat upon it in her splendid home and sipped tea, written letters, or read a novel. A decision had been made to part with the chair. He could imagine the hushed discussions, the conclusion, the resignation. There was sadness in all of it. Money was needed somewhere, for something, so a prized and precious chair was sent away to be sold. Any reminder of it was a reminder of loss. In doing his job well, he was doing harm in their eyes. The very job he had to do was the thing he must not do.

What could he say? It was a riddle and he had to solve it. His mind burned, turning it over and over. Why had they not given the chair to Hadley Brown, or another dealer, in the first place? Surely they knew there would be press, publicity, at Endicott's. They must have decided to endure all that at the outset, until it became too unpleasant. Then why? Why?

And then he had it. It was money. Endicott's had held

out the lure of a possible untold fortune to be gotten for the Cadwalader chair. It was a great gamble, a roll of the dice, and the stakes were fabulous. So simple. The answer had eluded him during the trip because one didn't think of the Peabodys, or anybody like them, needing money. They were like the Bank of England itself, or the Rockefellers. They were money, or were beyond it. But it was there, and as he examined his conclusion from every angle, it fit. He knew then what to say.

"Grace, no matter what price Hadley Brown's buyer has offered, Endicott's sale will bring double that amount!"

"Simon!"

"I'm sorry to put it that way, but I know parting with the chair is difficult, and you must have an important reason. Don't give up this opportunity to achieve the optimum price. All the work has been done. A dozen buyers are out there, all over the world, just waiting to outbid each other."

He jumped up and started pacing, gesticulating with his right hand. "Yes, we had a bit of a circus. But it's over, Grace. There are only three quiet months until the auction. Endicott's has been setting world records—you know that!—and the dealers are steamed up because the buyers are coming directly to us now, and we're doing better—yes, far better—for our consignors than the dealers have ever done. Please, don't succumb to Hadley Brown! The man is an...an opportunist." Simon spluttered out the last word and sank into his chair, his volley of persuasions exhausted.

Grace Peabody had drawn out a lace handkerchief, and she patted her mouth with it. Simon sensed the emotion working, and wondered what it would bring.

"But the...publicity...." The word was almost a whisper.

"No more, Grace. Just the traditional announcements that the sale is coming up. Oh, and a little article about me. No more than that." Simon leaned forward, solicitous. "You have my word."

She sat very quietly for a moment. When she spoke, it was with dignity. "Very well, Simon. I'll speak to Cartwright."

He leaped toward her and kissed her hand. "Thank you, Grace. Thank you."

It was only while driving home that night that he realized the bargain he had struck: to double the price of the chair at auction—not that he actually knew what Hadley Brown had offered—and to prevent further tawdry publicity. Was it in his power to do either of those things, let alone both?

※※※

The postcard screamed up at her, lying there among the photos and lithographs of Queen Anne tables she was cataloguing for the archives. It read:

> *Hi, Baby. South of France is great! Orchestra playing old favorites—the Bach Double et alia. How's the old furniture?*
> *Wish you were here.*
>   *Love,*
>   *N.*

Her cheeks flamed red, although she knew that Arabella, the deliverer of the missive, was watching her with interest. "Thanks."

She turned the card over quickly, revealing a scene of Provence. The address read Ms. Selena Fraccese, American Furnishings Department, Endicott's, 1680 Park Avenue, New York, N.Y. 10022 USA.

Arabella couldn't contain her curiosity. "So who's 'N.'?"

"A friend from school."

"Right." Arabella was unsatisfied, but Selena certainly wanted to go no further. She waited for the other girl to

95

return to her own desk and duties, which, after a little rummaging, she did.

How could he? She hated him.

She tried to return to the laborious business of the archives, but she was too deeply disturbed by the postcard and the avalanche of emotions it unleashed. She called to Arabella, "I'm going to the ladies' room for a moment."

"All right," Arabella said in return, and Selena wondered if she heard or imagined the tinge of knowing sarcasm in the response.

Whirling through the door to the lounge, which was large and well appointed for the use of Endicott's clients, she grabbed the vanity shelf and peered anxiously at herself in the mirror. Just as she feared. She looked flushed and ruffled. Her eyes were preternaturally bright. "Damn him, damn him, damn *it!*"

Endicott's was a nasty place behind the scenes, she'd decided early on, but she could handle all of it: being a lowly intern, having the snobbish, full-time employees snub her and put her down. Those arrogant young girls, brainless and shallow by her standards, were there because of social connections, their surnames, whom they knew. She was shocked, really shocked, at the breadth of their inabilities. Empty heads with specious art history degrees, good looks and fine pedigrees. Was this how things were decided in America? After a month she still couldn't quite believe their condescension to her and the other interns, their narcissistic interest in their appearance, haircuts, and clothing. And they didn't earn enough in a month to pay their clothing bills, let alone support themselves.

Still, she had a future, an excellent future. She knew it. This was a time for objectivity like no other. Resentment was beneath her. Endicott's was what it was: a stepping stone and a learning experience, and it certainly wasn't dull.

Yes, Endicott's she could handle. The situation with Neal was an entirely different matter—she could not apply the same logical analysis to it. As she tried to control her anger at Neal, she thought of Anna.

Thank God for Anna. An intern in the press department and a Columbia student, Anna had become lunch friends with Selena when they weren't "desk dining a la deli," as they called it. Selena splashed cold water on her eyes and returned to her working table. She called Anna's extension.

Anna answered with "Press department."

"Hi, it's Selena."

"Hi, what's up?" Anna's voice sunk to just above a whisper. There was no privacy in the press office, where the atmosphere usually ranged from rushing to pandemonium.

"Can you get out for lunch?"

"Hang on—I'll see." Selena heard the buzz in the backg round, then Anna's voice, barely discernible, saying, "Sidney, be a peach and do phones at lunch, puh-leeze?"

A rustle and a clank. "I can go at one; is that all right?"

"Good. I'll meet you in front." Selena was vastly relieved. Anna was a real person who cared about her work and professionalism, and she reminded Selena of her best friend at Wesleyan. Both girls seemed instinctively to understand the little hypocrisies and chicaneries of Endicott's without actually complaining or commenting on them, except by knowing glances.

Selena returned to her work, but her efforts were desultory and distracted. "South of France is great!" The letters on the card seemed etched before her eyes. And here she was in an organization not unlike a beehive, and she knew her position without a doubt. But the drudgery was finite: It would end. How she longed to soar, to have knowledge and position! Then, maybe, freedom. "South of France is great!"

But in the meantime....

Sighing a great deal, she watched the clock on her desk. It was 12:30. Then, after what seemed to be two hours, it was 12:50. She made ready slowly, gathering her tissues and the postcard, which she slipped into her purse after taking it from a drawer. Despite all the precautions of the coded lock system, there was still pilferage and petty theft at Endicott's. Behind the closed doors were both moving men and international millionaires, and one could expect such behavior when differing economic classes were in close proximity, just as they were in Manhattan itself.

She went down the long corridor, whooshed through reception, and slipped into the crowded little elevator. Somehow, Neal and Endicott's seemed incongruous; it was hard to think of him while she was within these walls. But he had intruded, had burst into her new world with the delicacy of a Roman candle. He was at Endicott's without being there at all. She held the purse containing the postcard. What she had to answer was whether or not he was in her heart, or whether there was any place for such a man in her heart or in the life she wanted for herself. Yes, she loved his smile, the warmth of him, the excitement; but she didn't want to be upset, on edge, dizzy, off center, as she always was with him. Such a life was unthinkable. She sighed. Better to talk this over with Anna, who seemed very level-headed, and someone who could understand Selena's own professional ambitions. Wise counsel—where did one find it?

Selena arrived out in front of the building first, nodding to the indefatigable James. Anna rushed out soon after.

"Sorry if I'm late—it's a zoo in there today. You look a bit peaky. Where are we going? Uncle Ha-Ha's Oriental House of Horrors, or Borscht Belt Kosher Pizza Heaven?" Selena smiled at her friend's unfailingly accurate descriptions of the eateries they frequented—a Chinese restaurant with a $3.95 lunch special, or Shecky's Pizza, several blocks further away.

"Let's do Uncle Hai's today—it's quieter." They fell into the quickened stride of the New Yorker. Selena decided to save her talk of Neal for the restaurant: she needed to be sitting down. "What's happening in Gossip Central today?" She used Anna's pet name for the press office.

"Selena, there's some big stuff afoot. I don't know all of it yet, but Walter Everest is going to be politely fired." Selena showed her surprise. Although Everest, the current president, was more of a totem or a figurehead, he was pleasant, well connected, and he seemed a competent administrator. Anna went on, "He's not one of Wunnicke's hand-picked people. Wunnicke inherited Walter when he took over, and he's been biding his time."

"How did you hear this? And how is someone 'politely' fired?" Selena's interest was suddenly focused on something other than Neal.

"Well...I can overhear Alex Putnam when he's on the phone. I can't help it, Selena, honestly! And when people come into his office and he doesn't close the door...." Anna lifted her shoulders in an exculpatory shrug.

"Go on, go on," Selena urged, but the street noise made it difficult for her to hear. They hastened through the July heat, anxious to gain entrance to another air-conditioned interior. There was a line, but a short one.

"Whew," said Anna, smiling. Fragrant scents drifted from the kitchen. The tables were small and crammed together. They sidled to the first available one, sat down and ordered two specials.

Anna went on. "Everest is being offered a transfer to some wicked outpost—Dubai or Singapore or some such. It's a sure bet he'll decline it. He'll have to—it's such an obvious step down."

"Wow," Selena whistled. "That's so sad. All that work and all the years of effort to attain a job like his, and to do it well, and then be fired for something that has nothing to do with your performance.... It doesn't seem quite fair, does it?"

"That's an understatement!" Anna voiced her agreement. "But that's not the half of it. Of course, there will be a new president named, probably soon. Mr. Wunnicke and the board are just waiting for the 'resignation' so it'll all look quite proper."

"How unpleasant," Selena replied. "Who do you think it'll be?

"I'm not sure, and I don't think Alex or Diana knows yet, either, but I've heard some rumors." Anna poured some tea and looked maliciously knowing.

"Well?"

"Sarah Dean, of course. Everybody thinks she's letting Wunnicke get into her pantyhose."

"Really?" Selena smiled at the picture in spite of herself. "Well, that's one way to get ahead."

"The *old* way," Anna added.

"She's really a very good businesswoman, Anna. It's a shame that, if she gets the presidency now, everybody will think she got it by being Wunnicke's mistress or whatever."

"Oh, no, he's got another mistress—and she's pregnant."

Selena dropped her spoon into her egg drop soup. "For heaven's sake, Anna! This sounds like an afternoon soap opera! I though he had a beautiful wife."

"He does."

"Well, then...?"

"Selena, my dear. Men like Wunnicke are about power. I think we can assume that with their insatiable drive for money and prestige come other insatiable drives, too. Wouldn't you think?" The two friends giggled.

"Who else is being considered for president?"

"Well, Harris Tompkins is another choice. He's been at Endicott's forever. His uncle was there before him, he knows everybody in the world, and he's the world's number one auctioneer." Anna said the last three words with a mock Chinese accent as she bit into a spring roll.

"He'd be a boring choice. Besides, president is an administrative job, not a performance one. Does he know enough about running the company?"

"Dear Seleen, is that ever a consideration at Endicott's?"

"I don't know. Is it?"

"But certainly not! Remember Laughlin Bradford, the Far Eastern arts head? He was just made marketing director last month with no experience whatsoever."

"But that's crazy!"

"That's Endicott's."

Selena poked at her rice with her chopsticks and sipped her tea. "Who else?"

"Last, but certainly not least, your dreamboat boss, the pin-up boy of the press department, Mr. Simon Haden-Jones." Anna sighed and clutched at her heart, making fake palpitations with her fist. "Bu-boom, bu-boom, bu-boom."

Selena flushed. Of course she knew her department head was attractive. She had felt the first stirrings of warmth for him when, after rescuing her, he had sat on the back of the intruder, looking quietly and steadily into her eyes. But she had attributed the feelings to the emotion of the moment. She was his employee, and the lowliest at that. He hadn't even chosen her—he had her foisted on him by her aggressiveness in getting the internship and the influence of her family name. He was unfailingly courteous and deferential, as was she, and he certainly kept his distance, as was proper.

Simon Haden-Jones, President of Endicott's?

When she found her voice, she said softly to Anna, "He'd be wonderful."

"Do you think so? How come?"

This time Selena blushed deeply.

"Oh, ho! So the proper Miss Selena has her little crushes, too."

"I don't at all. What nonsense! I just...respect him, that's all." She stammered over the word "respect." The conversation was taking a turn she didn't like.

"Wake up and smell the wonton, Selena-beana. You work for a guy who's gorgeous, rich, well-connected, and straight. In the art world, what more could you ask for? We're all so jealous of you! We work for cokeheads, fags, castrati, psycho-neurotics, pederasts, sadists, sycophants, and probably an ax murderer or two!" (Selena smiled.) "I ask you once again, what more could you want?"

Selena pushed her plate away from her. "Neal."

"Neal? Who the hell is Neal?"

She told Anna the story of the year-long campus affair, her intoxication with Neal, the thrill of the trysts, the deeply exciting sex. Anna listened earnestly. Then Selena drew out the postcard that had arrived that morning and handed it to her friend, saying simply, "I was supposed to be with him."

Anna looked at the postcard, front and back.

"Why did he send this, Anna? Why a postcard and not a letter? And why embarrass me by sending it to Endicott's? He could have found my address. He could have called. A postcard is so—public and impersonal. I don't understand."

Anna patted Selena's hand. Her friend's distress was so real that she pushed down an impulse to crack wise.

"You're not the first girl to have an affair with a professor, you know."

"I know."

"Do you want to know what I really think?"

Selena nodded vigorously.

"I think your Neal probably does this a lot."

"But why?"

"Because he's a professor. Because he—they—can. He's

around young, bright girls all the time. Selena, you're so very serious, and I'll just bet he isn't."

"But he said he loved me! We made plans together. Do men tell lies in bed, Anna? I don't even know that!"

"Yes, and they don't necessarily mean the same thing that you do when they say 'I love you'. And their sense of time—as in 'always'—seems to be quite different."

Selena pondered this. Anna continued, "He probably had a girl with him when he wrote this card to you."

"No, no, he wouldn't do that."

"Oh, yes, he would. It's a little game, Selena: keep the old lay on the string just in case the new one doesn't work out."

Selena was visibly shaken by the last statement, and spilled her tea as the little cup clattered into the saucer.

"I'm sorry, Seely, that sounded awful. But you must think tough. Don't let this guy upset you. After all, what would your prospects have been for the long run? You're not going to stay in Middletown, Connecticut. He's not marriage material."

"But...."

"No buts. Just forget about him. He knows how to rattle your chain, all right, and that's what he's doing." Anna picked up the postcard and tore it neatly in half.

Selena nodded. She wasn't happy, but she conceded that Anna had articulated thoughts that had been scuddering around somewhere in the back of her mind. Now she would think them through. They weren't very flattering ideas, but she would have to deal with them.

"Ready? Okay?" Anna asked. Selena nodded, and the two girls paid their checks and started back up the street to Endicott's.

"But Anna, why do I still feel so much when I think of him?"

"You're horny, my friend."

Simon awoke in the hours just before dawn, bathed in perspiration. He didn't want to come out of the dream. He resisted: No, not yet, take me back, hold me! But the dream was leaving him, caressing him with both hands, touching his body as it left, like a cloud dissipating before the sun. He lay in bed, somewhere between sleeping and waking, feeling beatified. He had never had such an exquisite sensation, and though he tried to catch the dream, it was gone now, distant, in gossamer shreds. His skin was alive, and his emotions were at a fever pitch. Although he was not at all religious, he thought of the ecstasy shining from the eyes of the saints and martyrs in the religious paintings of Botticelli. He thought they must have felt like this. He had seen Venus in his dream, but she wasn't Venus at all, but Selena, drifting in front of his eyes, ethereal. He remembered her face, so touched with beauty, and he was abashed to find that the thought of her was causing him to swell with an erection. Though it seemed improper, he couldn't help it.

He lay, enraptured, unwilling to move, trying to remember more of the dream. It had been about love, love that transcends the flesh but is of the flesh. He imagined that ethereal place between the clouds and the sun, so close to the ancient prophets' idea of heaven, beyond science, older than history, mythological.... It had been real to him in the dream. He had been there in the dream. With her.

He opened his eyes and stared into the blackness. The electricity in his body ebbed and he relaxed into the soft bed. The dream was about her, of course. Selena. He would wait no longer. He would make her his, and together they would go to the place in the dream. He would start today.

Chapter 13

"Dammit! Can't you fly this crate straight?" E. Martin Wunnicke yelled in annoyance at the closed cockpit door of his small private jet. The plane's lurch had caused wine to splash across the papers spread on the small conference table. Baron Moszinski smiled slightly, fingering his Waterford wine glass. "Damn wine cost me $275 a bottle at the London auction." Wunnicke was proud of the sums he spent on the collections of wine that came up for sale at Endicott's, and he never tired of reminding people of them.

"The von Freiberg auction, yes?" said the baron. Herbert Kazin, who never drank, said nothing.

"Miranda—remind me to get another pilot when we get back to Kansas City." The tall blond, beautifully dressed and coiffed, simply shrugged and crossed one long leg over the other. Her perception of her wifely duties differed from her husband's. She leafed through the latest issue of *Paris Vogue*.

"Now, gentlemen, where were we?" Wunnicke asked as he dabbed at the papers with a large, monogrammed napkin.

Kazin said, "About Everest's resignation."
"Oh, yes. The rest of the board has given us carte blanche on this, boys. They're not much interested in the day-to-day. Everest was notified in writing of his impending transfer to Dubai to find us 'wonderful treasures' and to 'create a presence' for us there." There was a knowing chuckle among the three men. "Of course, he called me and carried on about his goddamn contract. I told him his contract wasn't worth shit, and he was lucky I didn't dump him with a month's severance."

"Where does it stand now?" the baron inquired, uncomfortable with Wunnicke's scatological expletive.

"Oh, he'll quit, and soon. Has to save face with his clients and the dealers."

"Martin, I agree that Everest is not the man we want, but we must be careful to keep our reputation. As long as we stroll with Park Avenue, the other streets will follow, yes? Everyone else must come along. You do understand that, yes?" The baron stared at Wunnicke, making sure that his point was taken.

"My dear baron—Thad-yus—this won't cause a ripple, except maybe from Everest's mother. Believe me. We are about to go public. I have single-handedly—with the help of all the directors, of course—made this little operation fantastically profitable. No one is going to question my methods! Why should they? Everybody—I repeat, *everybody*—is making a bundle of money. Remember that guy who consigned the Leonardo drawing? He called me to thank me personally. He got ten times what he expected for the damn thing, and he's got a mother in a nursing home and a kid on drugs who needs to go into rehab. He's not going to question me. Nobody is." Wunnicke paused.

Herbert Kazin dropped two blue tablets into a glass and watched them fizz. "How's the ulcer, Herb?" Wunnicke boomed.

"Growing, thanks, Martin." Kazin internalized everything, while Wunnicke bludgeoned. Their styles, although complementary, were completely dissimilar, yet had brought both to fabulous wealth.

"I agree, Martin, with what you're doing: strengthening the management. I just ask you to be cautious." The baron looked from one man to the other.

"Well, thanks, Baron. I sure will. Now, about the matter of the new team."

The baron gave a thoughtful nod. In the back of the plane, Miranda Wunnicke, a former Miss Sweden, stifled a yawn and shifted her position. Her magnificent legs caught the eyes of all three men in the compartment.

"Ah, yes, the succession," the baron said, leaning forward to look at the organization chart Wunnicke had before him.

"There are three candidates for the job of president. I think you and Herb can name them."

Kazin said, "Harris Tompkins, of course," naming his favorite. He was circumspect and a conservative businessman.

Wunnicke nodded. "He's the perfect sop for the Old Guard. No change, and so forth. What do you think of him, Baron?"

Baron Moszinski closed his eyes and rolled his head back. "An uninspired choice. But safe, very safe. He is known well in Europe."

Wunnicke continued, "Then there's Sarah Dean." His voice betrayed no emotion or embarrassment, but Miranda Wunnicke's head shot up at the mention of the name. The *Paris Vogue* slipped from her fingers and fell to the floor with a thud. "She's the best business head we have, and she's ambitious and loyal." He allowed himself to think back to the recent evening when he had stood in the stacks among the antique violins and cellos and she was on her knees in front of him, playing him like an instrument, fingering him, bowing him to crescendo....

Kazin said, "Too young. And those clothes. Jogging shoes and little silk bow ties? Strictly Harvard Business School."

Wunnicke reddened, then checked himself. "Put her in some silk dresses and Paris suits, and she'll look fine, just fine. Why, the girl put together the whole stock offering practically by herself. It's so damn clever no one will ever figure out that we're selling 90% of the company and keeping 90% of the voting power. That's some kind of genius, in my book."

"A very talented young person," said the baron. "But there are difficulties. She has no art background at all, and as a young woman, she would be a problematical choice. Some Europeans, and the Asians especially, don't like to see a woman in an executive role. We must think of them; they are a large part of our business now."

"You're right about that," Wunnicke conceded.

"Have you anyone else in mind, Martin?" Kazin asked quietly.

"Yes, but let me come back to it. It just occurred to me that there's another change I want to make. I want to can the Jew who's setting up the credit card operation for us."

"But why?" the baron asked. "I hear he does an excellent job."

"He does, but we don't need him any more. Sarah can handle it from here, and I don't like the guy. He wears a beard and red suspenders, for Chrissakes! I don't care if he's from Unibank, he's just not the Endicott's type."

"Bernard Schwartzman? Is that his name?" Kazin asked. "Doesn't he have a three-year contract with us?"

"So what?" Wunnicke boomed. "What's the guy gonna do, sue us? We can always find cause or a loophole in his contract. Getting rid of him won't be a problem."

"Careful, Martin," the baron admonished.

"Why should I buy a goddamn company if I can't run it?" Wunnicke banged a fist on the table. "We'll have an Endicott's credit card soon. The most prestigious platinum card in the world. We don't need Schwartzman any more. I'm getting rid of him."

The baron lifted his hands in helpless acquiescence. He knew when to back off. Wunnicke's mind was made up, and the baron liked his position of power and prestige as a member of the inner circle of Endicott's Board of Directors,

108

even if he knew he was chosen for his family's name and fabulous art collection. Arnold Schwartzman didn't count in the larger scheme of things.

"Let's speak again about the presidency," he urged, noting the throbbing vein at Wunnicke's left temple.

"Yes," said Wunnicke, knowing he had won the skirmish. "Let me tell you who I've been thinking about." The two men looked at him with interest. Miranda sighed and turned the page of the magazine. "Simon Haden-Jones."

"Please?" the baron asked.

"You know, that tall guy who talked to us about the Catwaller chair last spring at the board meeting? Head of American Furniture or some damn thing?"

Kazin took out a roll of pink digestive tablets and began to chew on one. Both men waited for Wunnicke to speak again. "He's the right kind of guy to be president. Rich, good-looking, knows his stuff. The ladies will love him, and the men will respect him. He's made us a lot of money, brought in old families, sold high. He's class." Wunnicke stopped.

"But he's not a businessman," Kazin commented.

"Don't—doesn't matter. We have Sarah, who's got enough brains for five businessmen."

"What about Sarah?" Kazin asked. "Will she stay if she's passed over?"

"Oh, she'll stay." Wunnicke smiled to himself as if at a private joke. "I'll explain to her that she's a little too young now, but we're grooming her. I'll make her Haden-Jones' executive vice president. She'll be fine." Privately, Wunnicke had decided he'd do a few other things for Sarah Dean—a quiet trip to Paris for clothes, and a larger apartment. But he didn't share that decision with the other men, or with his wife.

"That would leave a problem that you Americans would

say is 'sticky,'" the baron said. "What about Mr. Tompkins?"

"We need him. He's Mr. Endicott's," Kazin added.

"He's a buffoon," Wunnicke snorted.

"It doesn't matter, Martin. You can't cut him out. He won't be content to stay as auctioneer when others are promoted above him."

Wunnicke thought for a moment. "What do you suggest, Herb?"

"Give him some highfalutin' title, a raise, and get your PR guy to ghostwrite a book by him and put him all over the media looking like the world's greatest authority on something or other. Dishes. Statues. Whatever. Tompkins is a reasonable man. He'll accept it."

"Thanks for your input, Herb. I think I can formalize all of this at the next board meeting. If you have any more thoughts, please let me know privately. Otherwise, I'd appreciate your speaking to the other directors and convincing them of the wisdom of these decisions."

The pilot's voice came over the loudspeaker. "We'll be experiencing some turbulence while landing, Mr. Wunnicke."

"Goddamn pilot," muttered Wunnicke as he drained the last of the wine from the von Freiberg auction and fastened his seat belt.

XOXOX

Times Square at night. Freddie walked back and forth on a single block of 43rd Street, averting his eyes from the human detritus oozing out of doorways and subway exits. Orange and green lights shone and intermingled in the puddles left by an afternoon rain. Cacophonous sound drifted out of the doorways of bars and strip joints. The theatre crowd had departed. A homeless man in reeking clothes stumbled up to Freddie.

110

"Hey, man, my old lady just had a baby and I need a dollar for bus fare to go see her. Can you help me out?"

"Imaginative, but obviously untrue. Be off, my good fellow," Freddie said decisively, and strolled a little faster. He could see the light in Duane's little window. He knew he was there. Despite the heat and the growing number of street people, he decided to wait another half hour.

Suddenly, the light went off. Freddie tensed and watched the narrow front door of the building, sandwiched between a souvenir shop and the Pink Pussycat Bar. Then he saw the door open, and the young man, clad in jeans and a T-shirt and carrying a large dance bag, came out.

Freddie crossed the street, dodging taxicabs, and came up behind the hurrying figure. As he fell into stride with the young man, he turned, tipped his Homburg, and said, "Fancy meeting you here!"

The boy gave him a quick look and said, "Oh, hullo, Freddie."

Freddie was happy just to be near him, to be walking down the street with him on a hot July night. He asked the boy, "Do any auditions today?" The boy hurried on in silence.

"Want to come to my place for a drink, Duane?"

The boy stopped cold and said, "*Don't ever call me Duane! My name is Dimitri. Got that? Dimitri.*" He turned away from Freddie and broke into a trot. Stricken, Freddie ran along behind.

"Please, Dua—Dimitri. I miss you. I've got to see you."

"Look, Freddie. I've got a job tonight. I'm booked practically every night. I told you. Be a good guy, OK? Leave me alone. If you want to see me, call Wilhelm."

Freddie's pride was scalded. "I do not call pimps," he said quietly.

Duane stopped and faced him. "Wilhelm is not a pimp!

111

He's my manager."

"Manager, indeed. Don't you see he's just using you to make money for himself? He's not interested in you!"

"You're wrong. He gets us dates with lots of producers, directors, and agents. They all see us dance. Tonight we're going to do our act for a lot of Hollywood bigwigs. You're making me late, so bug off, Freddie."

"Wait, Dua—Dimitri, please!" He caught desperately at the young man's arm. "Have you ever gotten a dancing job through Wilhelm? Ever?"

"Sure! I got two weeks at Chippendale's in May."

"Chippendale's!" Freddie snorted. "That's not dancing. You should be with a company. You should be dancing with Ballet Theater, or the New York City Ballet, or Paul Taylor!"

"Hey, look. I like you. You're a nice guy. But I pay for my room and my classes working for Wilhelm, and I'm going to make it big. I'm gonna be a big star."

"Oh, Duane," Freddie whispered. (How could he answer that insane fantasy?) "Come live with me. I'll pay for your classes. And I'll introduce you to important people."

"Sure, sure, those upper class fags who go on and on about their ashtrays, and the bored old dames? No, thanks."

"Then just let me see you, please. Just for fun." He tried to sound nonchalant, but even to his own ears he sounded desperate.

"Can't. You've got to call Wilhelm." The boy turned abruptly and sprinted across 47th Street toward the East Side. Freddie dropped back and leaned against a building. He was silent for a moment, then his lips pulled tight against his teeth in a grimace of pain, and he began to sob, quietly at first, then with breaking gasps. Tears rolled down his face as he stumbled down the street. A homeless woman looked at him, then thought better of approaching him with her latest tale of woe.

Chapter 14

The next day at Endicott's was a busy one for Simon. The pace was accelerating toward the fall auctions, with the sale of the Cadwalader chair an international event. The chair was to be the subject of an Endicott's poster, and was the highlight of the fall sale brochure. Superb photographs were imperative, and there were a million attendant details. He wasn't able to think about Selena, or about his resolution of the early dawn, until the close of the business day, when he feared she might have already left. Just as he pushed back his chair and leaned towards the telephone, it rang.

"Simon? Alex Putnam here."

"Hello, Alex."

"You remember the *House & Garden* thing?"

Simon had never felt at ease with Alex Putnam; something bothered him about the man's manner with him. He could never put his finger on it, nor did he ever take time to worry about it. "Of course I remember it. They were photographing my apartment for the better part of two days."

"Oh, yeah. Well, the writer, Letitia Granby, wants to talk to you again to clarify some quotes. They're right at deadline. Can you meet her for drinks?"

"Now?" Letitia Granby had continually grabbed his knee while interviewing him. He didn't care to fend her off again. "Alex, I've had an awful day, and I'm really not up to Letitia Granby tonight."

"Well, Mr. Wunnicke seems awfully keen about this piece getting run on time." Alex's emphases on Wunnicke's name and "on time" were unmistakable.

Simon sighed. "Yes, of course. Well...could I meet her for an early breakfast tomorrow instead? Near her office? At 8?"

"Just a minute, I'll see." He put Simon on hold. "She says all right; the Pierre at eight."

"Fine."

Alex hung up without good-byes or ceremony, cutting off Simon's "Thank you." Strange bird, Simon thought, and he again reached for the phone and pressed the number for Selena's extension. After four rings, he was about to give up when he heard her breathless voice.

"American Furniture."

"Selena, it's Mr. Haden-Jones. Could you come in for a moment, please?"

"Of course."

She appeared at the door, looking slightly disheveled and not at all like Botticelli's *Venus*, with a charming small purse dangling from her shoulder and a carrying case in her hand.

"Come in, please, and sit down. Am I keeping you from something?"

"Oh, no, nothing at all." She sat prettily in the same chair in which he had first welcomed her on her first day—was it just seven weeks ago?

"I trust you received your mail?"

Selena blushed deeply, realizing that he must have seen the scarlet postcard from Neal. It was an agony for her, who had been brought up to observe the utmost discretion and finesse in such matters. "Yes, I did, thank you." She could scarcely look at him, not realizing how harmless the message was to the casual reader. Simon had not even glanced at it.

"How are you enjoying your work in our department?"

"The department is extraordinary, and I like it very much, Mr. Haden-Jones."

"Do you think...would you feel comfortable calling me Simon?"

114

She smiled and released a little breath. "Thank you—I'll try, Mr....Simon."

Simon thought he was handling the situation rather badly. Even though he knew that he couldn't close the door, enfold her in his arms, kiss her, and bury his face in her chestnut hair, he knew as well that he shouldn't sound like a principal interviewing a star student.

"I want to thank you, Selena. You see how busy we are. I don't think we—I—could've managed without you."

Selena beamed with pleasure. It was the first word of gratitude she had received in the little universe called Endicott's, the first recognition for the thankless hours of hard toil.

Simon continued, "I know that the archives are awful—and boring—but they're invaluable to us. I've tried employees and temps before, and they never seem to do them right. I've looked at your work and it's...well, it's perfect. Thank you very much."

Selena wouldn't have traded this moment for anything.

"Are you planning to go on in the auction field?" Simon was running out of legitimate things to say in the makeshift interview, and knew he must soon come to the point.

"No, I want to be in museums, a curator or museum head, I hope. Eventually." Her beautiful eyes rested on him.

"Look, we've both had a long day, and it's getting hotter than blazes in here." Endicott's shut off its air-conditioning to the offices promptly at five. "I'd like to hear more about your plans. Are you free for dinner on Friday?" The fatal words were out. He hadn't felt so nervous or generally idiotic since he'd asked Tabby Auckland to his first school dance. What if she said no? But she wouldn't. She would say yes, but for the wrong reasons. Because he was her boss. Because he had couched his initiative in suitable professional terms. Well, he'd have to worry about that later. He could think of no other way to start.

Selena's head shot up. She was astonished by the invitation. Had he really asked her to dinner? Dinner?

"Pardon me?"

"Friday night. Dinner—are you free?" Simon suddenly wished he hadn't asked. He could sense her confusion. After a long moment, she said, "Thank you. I am free for dinner on Friday."

)O(O(O(

"Friday? *Friday?* Where's he taking you? What are you wearing? Oh, my God, Friday! *Simon Haden-Jones?*"

"For heaven's sake, Anna, it's dinner, not a trip to Mars."

Loretta, who had been sitting cross-legged on the floor of Selena's apartment sketching clothing designs on her oversized white pad, started chanting under her breath, "Thank God it's Friday, thank God it's Friday, thank...."

"Lorry, you are breaking my concentration!" Julio held a play script in one hand, and was throwing himself with brute force against the wall again and again. "*Ow!*"

"What happened, honey bunch?" Loretta scrambled up and embraced Julio, who was ineffectually trying to kiss his own shoulder.

"And quarterbacks think *they* have it rough."

Loretta snapped her fingers. "Hey, that's a great idea! Shoulder pads! I think my kid brother has some."

Julio gave her a withering glance.

"What is this play about, anyway, Julio?" Selena asked.

"Drug addicts and narcs, what else? I'm practicing my wrongful arrest." Julio resumed flinging himself against the wall, this time leading with the other shoulder. Loretta, her concentration interrupted, turned her attention to Selena and Anna. "A date, huh? What are you going to wear?"

116

"Oh, I hadn't thought about it...."

"This guy's your boss, huh? Pretty old? So you don't want to look sexy. That could be dangerous."

"No, not old," Selena said. "He's under forty—what do you think, Anna?"

"He's 37. Divorced. A Yale graduate. Family goes back to Plymouth Rock, the part that's not still in England."

"How do you know all this?" Selena asked in genuine amazement.

"Press files, silly! We have bios on, and photos of, everybody who's anybody at Endicott's."

"Divorced? I wonder why? He's not the sort of man anyone would leave."

"Lots of money, huh?" Loretta asked in complete innocence. "*Julio!* You're going to break the plaster!"

Anna took Loretta's lead. "Oh, he's got more than money, believe me. He's semi-gorgeous, Loretta. A little too tall for my liking, and I suppose he's a bit less macho than a rodeo cowboy, but he'll do."

Selena flushed. She hadn't thought of Simon in an objective way, and was surprised that she was so interested in Anna's information. "Well, Miss Anna-knows-everything, what happened to his marriage?"

"Come into the kitchen. I want some instant." The two girls moved ten feet to the alcove that served as the kitchen.

"Hey!" Loretta scrambled to her feet. "I want to hear, too."

"There was a real tragedy. He and his wife, Miss Muffy Gotrocks or whatever, had a baby son, and he was killed in a car accident. The marriage didn't survive after that. She had affairs, and married some jet setter right after the divorce."

"Poor man." Selena was deeply touched by the story. "Maybe that's why he always seems to be working."

"My sources say that the working late started before the marriage broke up, not after."

117

"Yes? Well, it's still terribly sad."

Loretta held up a sketch of an outré garment with a hat that looked for all the world like a giant inverted tea strainer. "What do you think?"

Anna giggled. Selena answered "Very interesting...for the right person. You, for example, Lorry." The kettle whistled and they all broke into peals of laughter.

"I'll have lemonade," Julio called from the living room.

"Nice try, Lambsie, but there's only coffee or tea." Loretta poked her head through the opening to the living room.

"Never mind me, then." A stage sigh issued from him.

"Don't mind him. He's spoiled rotten. I love him—his mother loves him—Shecky loves him—his coach loves him.... Oh, my gosh, you two probably love him, too!"

"*We do!*" they choroused. Lorry beamed at her friends.

"Now, Selena, be serious." Loretta grabbed Selena's arm, tugging her toward the closet behind the kitchen. "You have to wear something very special. Come on—let's see what you have." She marched to the closet, ignoring Selena's "I didn't bring very much...." and began rifling through the clothes.

"No, no, maybe, hmm, *no*, possible, no, no, *yes!*" She pulled out a black linen sundress with multiple bias straps across the back. "Oh, *madre mia*, feel that boning—this dress is *built*." Fumbling for the label, she read: "Gee—ven—chee, Givenchy! He's a genius. He's an architect, he constructs. I bow down to him!" Loretta fell reverently to one knee and blessed herself.

"That's sacrilegious, Lorry," Anna said.

"You're right. I forgot myself. Selena, this is *it*. Hold it up against you. Great! Okay, what shoes? What'll you do about your hair? How about jewelry?"

"For heaven's sake, Loretta, I haven't thought about it at all." Selena blushed furiously. The attention to her dress was making her nervous, and she didn't want to be.

"But you don't have to think. The couturier is here! What time are you going?"

"I suppose about eight o'clock—after work."

"Okay, you can call me and let me know. I'll be here a half hour before you go, and I'll fix your hair. And don't worry about jewelry. I'll help you with your accessories."

Loretta left the room to show the black dress, which she held as one might carry a precious tapestry, to Julio.

"Oh, dear," Selena sighed. Visions of the tea strainer hat with pigeon feathers sticking out from each hole in the mesh suddenly danced before her eyes. "Oh, dear."

"Don't worry, Seely. The dress is a dream, and you're so pretty. If you don't like what Loretta does to you, you can undo it quickly enough. Let her try. She want wants to help you so much."

Selena nodded, and gave a little helpless gesture. She sank against the frame of the closet door. "What'll I do with Mr. Haden-Jones, Anna? What'll I say?"

"You'll listen and respond. You'll smile. Don't *worry* about it. I wish I had such a problem. And for God's sake, *call me!* I can't wait all weekend to hear what happened." Anna looked at Selena's closet. "What's in those notebooks? You didn't bring class notes here with you, did you?"

"No."

"Then what?"

"My writing. It helps me use English better."

"What kind of writing?"

"It's nothing, just poetry."

"*Just* poetry? You write, too? Excuse me, I'll just go out and shoot myself now. Could I read something?"

"It's quite...personal."

"Not 'Ode on an Italian Fern' or anything like that? Oh, no. It's not about that guy, is it? That Neal?"

"Some of it."

119

"Well, I think that's probably in the past, don't you?"
Selena nodded.

"When you feel like showing it to me, do. I *love* poetry, the mushier the better." Selena looked sad, and Anna quickly changed the subject. "Let's go out for some frozen yogurt. It's summer in the city!" She started for the living room, calling to Julio and Loretta, "Do you guys want to get some yog...hey—is that kissing in the play?"

An hour later, Selena returned to the apartment alone, and walked to the closet. After a long moment, she selected a notebook. Opening it at random, she looked at the page. Funny how childlike her handwriting looked, making soft columns down the lined paper. Funny. Her handwriting couldn't have changed, could it? She read:

You are elemental.
Earth, wind, fire,
As blinding as light.

The frisson of electrified air
Is where you walk.
Stars tangle in your hair.

The laser of your mind
Leaps and burns, and turns....

She closed the notebook quietly, without finishing the verse. You. Who was "you," anyway?

Chapter 15

Sarah Dean strode down the curving second-floor corridor of Endicott's, shoulders bumping against the walls and the framed Picasso and Degas reproductions boasting of record prices achieved. She turned abruptly into the foyer of the executive office suite, nearly colliding with the secretary, Franca. "Sorry, Frank," she murmured without missing a beat or looking at the girl. She walked into her office and closed the door behind her. Something felt wrong. She was bothered, on edge, and couldn't put her finger on it. Was it Simon Haden-Jones? His utter contempt when she had told him about the reserve policy? No, she had steeled herself to that sort of response years ago. Women who wanted to make it to the top had to flex their muscles, had to be tough. Her policies were making a fortune for the company; they were, therefore, the right and appropriate policies. There was no other measure. Soft people like Simon Haden-Jones could afford to be principled and high-minded. Haden-Jones could, if he chose, spend the rest of his life splitting hairs, eyeing old furniture, and studying obscure teacups. He had a trust fund. Sarah had her brains and her guts. She'd come this far using them, and she would prevail.

"This department does not need to stoop to your dictum, Miss Dean," he had said before turning his back on her. Dictum! What kind of word was that, anyway? Well, they would see.

No, Haden-Jones was a minor annoyance. What was putting her on edge was some feeling in the air. Her last conversation with Wunnicke had been a little inconclusive, somehow. He'd said nothing in particular, but she sensed he had something to say, something he was holding back. She slammed her attaché case down on the desk, sat down, and began tapping a pencil against the desk top, rat-a-tat-tat. She would soon be president of Endicott's; she knew that. Then she would have more control. Her position would be unassailable, inviolable. Walter Everest's resignation would come any day now. The signs were unmistakable.

Walter had closeted himself in his office, and only appeared, looking ashen, coming in in the morning, and going out at night after most of the staff had left. The constant light on his line attested to the number of phone calls he was making. She'd seen it all before: executives who were being terminated desperately trying to find something else, another position, before their world fell in. Poor Walter. She almost felt sympathy for him. The auction world was so small, so tight, that his chances of moving laterally were close to zero. But it wasn't her problem—the balance sheets were.

Wunnicke would be in town tomorrow for a reception. He'd have that smiling, silent kewpie doll of a wife on his arm. She didn't care. Miranda Wunnicke was like the hood ornament on her husband's Rolls-Royce. Only she, Sarah Dean, was a match for Wunnicke. It would be all right. Her unease, she reasoned, was just because it was so close to the wire. So much was about to happen. She'd never been a patient girl; why should she be a patient woman? Usually she felt exhilaration at the kill, at the climax of the battle, when her beautifully orchestrated plans fell into place and she triumphed. Why not now? Why this nagging worry?

She'd talk to Wunnicke tomorrow night about speeding things up, hastening Everest's departure. There would be so much to do when she took over. She had great plans. One of them involved Simon Haden-Jones. She couldn't wait.

Simon worried about where to take Selena now that he'd asked her. Raffington's wasn't possible; the gossip that would follow an appearance there would embarrass them both. He had to look beyond the comfortable little ring of clubs and restaurants he frequented. It was challenging. It was impossible. Again, the sense of how little he knew the city in which he lived and worked assailed him. An Italian restaurant? Ridiculous! She was from Italy, and might be offended. Ethnic? He didn't know any, and the cuisine might be terrible. Chinatown? Too déclassé.

This puddling was getting him nowhere. At last, he decided to ring Freddie, who might have a solution to his problem. He picked up the receiver and pushed the buttons.

"Freddie Trowbridge."

Hearing the familiar voice quieted Simon's nerves, and he let out a breath. "Hello, Freddie—or, as they say in your department, *ça va?*" Simon's French accent was pure North Umbrian to Freddie's ear, and he laughed. His friend's talents were decidedly not in languages.

"Simon, my dear *copain*. What a pleasant tingle on a soupy day!"

"Making money—excuse me, francs—hand over fist?"

"Nothing so crass. Remember, we're Bronte's, where art is pure, and where no Valkyrie leads us up the slippery slopes of the Mount of Money."

"How silly of me to forget." Freddie's colorful persiflage always made him laugh. "Look, I have a little...situation that's come up."

"Dear *Dieu*, not The Chair again!"

"No, no. It's that I...well...I seem to find myself with a date for dinner, and I have no idea where to take her."

"But that's stupendous, *mon ami*. It's about time. Who's

the lucky demoiselle?"

"Well, that's a problem, too. It's my departmental intern."

There was a prolonged silence, which seemed to Simon to last a decade. When Freddie spoke, it was in a hoarse whisper. "I am *etonné*, I am *concassé*, I am...darn surprised at you, Simon. You never went in for robbing the cradle."

"It's not like that. She's a lovely girl from Italy. In fact, you may know her father, the Duce di Fraccese?"

There was a loud crash and what sounded like general mayhem at the other end of the line. "Freddie, are you there? What happened?"

"I just fell off my *chaise de bureau*, Simon. Hmmm. Let me recap the information you've just imparted: a student—your intern—and an Italian whose father is a player in the international art market. Have your gone stark raving *mad* in your posh little corner of Endicott's? To say this is not politic is the understatement of the year!"

"All right, all right." Simon cut him short. "This seems unwise, improper, and maybe downright stupid to me, too. But I just can't help it. She's...very special."

"I see." Freddie sensed the emotion in Simon's words. Maybe Simon felt for this girl what he felt for Duane, although he devoutly hoped not. Who was he to judge? His own passion was bringing him a pain he had not believed possible. "Well, I see your situation. You *can't* be seen with her. But you *can't* go to your place. And you *can't* go just anywhere, because she's used to a certain level. What a lot of *can'ts!* Let me think...hmmm.... Break the date, *mon ami*."

"Come on, Freddie. Help me with this."

"Joe's Clam House in Red Hook, New Jersey?"

"Freddie!"

"Give me two minutes to compose myself. I am in ten pieces at the moment. I'll ring you right back." Freddie sighed and shook his head as he hung up.

124

Simon wondered if he'd been mistaken in asking Freddie's help. He certainly did not need censure from his best friend. The phone rang, and Simon grabbed at it.

"I've got it, I've got it! And I am persuaded to give it to you to save you from utter ruin. The Waldorf. Peacock Alley. You'll *never* see anyone you know, the room's pretty *and* tucked away, the food is passable, and they have some crooner who tinkles away in the background on Cole Porter's old piano."

"That sounds fine, just fine."

"Oh, Simon. You could wear an eye patch and paint on a moustache. Just in case."

"Goodbye, Freddie—and thanks. Thank you very much."

"*De rien, mon ami, de rien.* Have fun." Freddie hoped that his tone was light. His heart was not.

※※※

Simon arrived five minutes early on Friday. He was completely unprepared for how she looked. How could she look like that? All day at Endicott's she'd had her hair loose, and her sleeveless blouse revealed smudges on her forearms where she'd delved into the stacks. She had been wearing the shapeless canvas flats that the interns favored that summer, and her air had been professional and disciplined. They had hardly spoken. So how could she possibly look as she did now?

He had mounted the stairs to her building feeling rather giddy and debonair. Now that the details of the evening were arranged, he felt quite carefree. He was going to be with her, and her alone, and he felt wonderful. Somehow, he thought they might have fun. It was summer in New York, he was a bachelor with an enviable position at a world-renowned company, and he was taking a lovely girl out to

125

dinner. Other people did it all the time. Even the heat of July seemed sensuous, lulling.

She had appeared at her door in the simplest black dress, and in high heels, which made her seem much taller. It was her hair that caught his eye. It was done in an upsweep that made her look like a figure in a painting by Sargent. Around her face, a simple band of black feathers curled from one ear around to the white hollow of her throat. A tiny diamond earring glittered in each ear.

"Hello. You look beautiful."

"Thank you." She felt shy, but she decided the compliment from Simon was sincere. Loretta's dyed pigeon feather hat, devised especially for Selena, was a success. She had known it the moment she looked in the mirror.

"Loretta—this is terrific! It's so simple and understated."

"But of course it is. It's just like you—and Mr. Givenchy."

Selena had given her friend a quick hug, then returned to the image in the mirror, tucking the last black feather into place.

"Now, Selena—have fun. This is your first date in New York!"

"I'll try, Loretta. I *will* try." She waved good-bye as Loretta let herself out.

And now Simon stood at her door, only minutes later. She hesitated about asking him in, decided against it. She smiled, took her small purse from the bookcase, went out and closed the door behind her, locking the several bolts.

"Are you hungry?" Simon asked as he took her elbow, guiding her to the small elevator.

"A little. The heat makes me not want to eat very much."

"It is strange, isn't it? If we stay in air conditioning all day, we're ravenous. But as soon as one hits the street and the heat...." Simon guided her toward the Mercedes, which was parked in front of a hydrant.

"Is this your car? It's wonderful." She ran an appreciative hand across the dull green fender as Simon opened the passenger door for her, helped her in, then ran around the front to be in the driver's seat as quickly as possible.

"Do you like it?" he asked as he signaled to pull out.

She nodded. "My father has an old Lamborghini Miura that he adores. What a pet he's made of it! Neither my brother or I was ever allowed to drive it, and riding in it was a special treat." She gazed around the interior of the Mercedes. "Does your top come down?"

"Yes, but I usually only take it down in the country. New York worries me. I guess I expect to be pelted by slops."

"Slops?" She asked, puzzled.

"Garbage," he said.

"Oh, yes, garbage." She was silent as he headed across 83rd to Lexington. "Do you think there will be 'slops' tonight?"

He laughed aloud at her ingenuousness, laughed with the sheer pleasure of being in Aunt Georgina's Mercedes with a wonderful woman, a woman he loved and wanted. "No, I think Lexington Avenue will be safe. Would you like the top down? It may blow your hat a bit."

"Yes, please."

Simon pulled over at a bus stop, lowered the top and secured it manually. As he pulled back into traffic, she sighed with pleasure. "This is a way I haven't seen New York. It's like starry canyons."

"Yes, isn't it?" The warm air moved in and around them, making little eddies. Selena dropped her head back against the tan leather, staring up at the architectural profiles in the deep twilight. The black feathers moved gently against her throat. Simon felt constricted with love, insanely happy. He thought, please let me hold this moment, let me live in it a while....

They drove slowly down Lexington Avenue, past coffee shops, boutiques, and bookstores. She grew more and more at ease. The hot summer night cast a sultry spell. The city seemed almost deserted; everyone who could leave had gone to the country or the beach. Taxis plied for fares, their drivers casting languid glances at the couple in the old Mercedes convertible. Just beyond 49th Street, Simon pulled over to the curb. "Please go in to the lobby, and I'll meet you in a moment." He walked around the car to open the door for her.

"Oh, the Waldorf! I remember we stayed here once when I was small."

He felt a pang of insecurity. "I hope you liked it." She nodded yes. "Good, good. Now, just wait for me at the top of the escalator."

He pulled the car around the corner and into the garage, and walked quickly back to the entrance. She stood at the top of the escalator, looking intently at a piece of carved jade in a jeweler's window. He realized then that he loved her mind, which was restless and constantly evaluating what passed before her lovely eyes.

"It's not very good, is it?" she asked, turning to him with a smile.

"No, it isn't," he said, once again taking her arm and leading her along the thickly carpeted corridor.

They made a stunning couple as they walked into the central lobby, though neither was aware of it. Selena, with her dark hair, patrician bearing, and fair skin set off by the black she wore; and Simon, tall and fit in a beige linen suit. Tourists looked at them as they passed. As they reached Peacock Alley, the maître d', smiling and unctuous, said, "Yes, sir?"

"Two for dinner, please. Haden-Jones."

"This way, sir."

The room was mirrored, dim, and cool. They were seated at a small table, Simon making sure that Selena had a view of the piano, which was intricately inlaid with marquetry. "Is this all right?"

"Yes, perfect. What a lovely piano."

"It belonged to Cole Porter. Do you know him?"

"But of course! *La Notte e Dia*—like the beat, beat, beat of the tom-tom.

"Yes—those lyrics. I've always been impressed with his internal rhyme schemes."

"Wasn't he a genius at that! Let's see—nimble tread of the feet of Fred Astaire."

Freddie, I thank you, Simon thought. Just right. The waiter appeared. "May I suggest the tournedos, sir?" They both ordered that entree, with green salads, and Simon chose a Beaujolais he felt was light enough for the heat that would assault them as they left the venerable hotel. Left. He never wanted to leave. As they dined, a pianist began to play and sing ballads, love songs, show tunes. It was pleasant and moody, redolent of the old clubs of the forties.

"If you really like Cole Porter, you must hear Bobby Short at the Cafe Carlyle. He's on vacation now, but I'd love to take you to hear him in the fall."

"I'll be back at school in Connecticut, I'm afraid." She smiled and dropped her eyes.

Simon was suddenly aware of time, how little time there was. "Will you be in New York when the Cadwalader chair comes up?"

"I'm not sure. My sublet is over on Labor Day, and I was planning to go back to Wesleyan then."

Simon felt a wave of despair. To find her and to lose her again in the space of a brief summer seemed cruel punishment. He didn't want her to leave him or be away from him, ever. But she had her own life, her own plans, in which he didn't even figure. At least, not yet.

All through dinner she spoke of her desire to be a museum curator, "probably in Europe," and to be a learned and influential one. She wanted to write books that would make people feel as she felt about the great works of man. He watched her face as she talked, its animation, its various expressions. The raven-black frame of feathers seemed to him like an earthly halo. He wasn't concentrating on what she said.

"But what about you?" she asked, and he had to stir himself. "There's a lot going on at Endicott's, isn't there. You've been there a long time?"

"Thirteen years. It's been completely engrossing. Things are different since Martin Wunnicke bought us, but it hasn't affected me particularly, or my department." He shrugged off the nagging memory of Sarah Dean's new reserve policy.

She looked at him intently. "Don't you think it might?"

"You know, Selena, I haven't given it much thought. I wanted to build my department, and Endicott's, into the world's best. I've devoted myself to that for many years. And since I acquired the Cadwalader, I feel that I've achieved what I was trying to do. Dealers around the world look to us for pricing and vetting and provenances. We've almost never been wrong. I'm proud of that."

"You should be. But what will you do next?"

"Oh, take on another department or two, I suppose. I'm pretty good at rugs and Victoriana."

Selena struggled with the urge to ask him if he knew he was being considered for the presidency. She knew she must not. He would wonder how she knew, and she couldn't compromise Anna. From what he'd said, he had no burning desire to be president of Endicott's. She wondered how the succession scenario would unfold, and rather hoped that she would be around to see the internecine drama. She decided to change the subject.

"Why is the Cadwalader chair so special? It doesn't look much different from some of the other American Chippendale chairs we have."

"No, it doesn't. Of course, the details of the workmanship are exquisite. But there's something else, a kind of magical quality. You feel it in a museum, sometimes, when you look at a work from ancient Egypt or Sumer or Babylonia—a vessel or a piece of jewelry that has seen the whole of the drama of human history. It has witnessed birth, death, royal intrigues, love affairs, murders. It holds the whole human story within itself, and it carries it through time to us. The Cadwalader is like that. It has that quality. And it's been loved almost to death."

Selena laughed at the odd expression. "What do you mean?"

"Would you like me to show you?"

"Now?

"Yes, if you've finished." She held up a spoon with a tiny trace of chocolate mousse, and smiled. Simon motioned for the check.

They walked through the vast lobby and went out of the hotel into the subtropical New York night. Selena insisted on accompanying Simon to the garage, where they waited in silence for the Mercedes. As he opened the door for her he said, "You'll find Endicott's interesting at this hour."

She wondered. Back to work on a Friday night seemed less than interesting, somehow. They drove across 50th Street to 1st Avenue, and then uptown, the hot breezes playing about their heads and shoulders, the occasional blast from a passing radio startling them. Simon found a metered spot directly in front of the auction house.

"You see? Distinct advantages." They went to the door,

where Simon signaled to the night guard, who opened the door and said, "Good evening, sir. Back again?"

"Yes, Al, back again."

Selena smiled at the guard and stepped inside the double glass doors. The building was profoundly still, lit only by a few corridor lights. The air was stale. "Do you often come in at night?" she asked.

"Not in the summer, but in winter I do. It's a wonderful opportunity to work without interruption, and to read." She wondered fleetingly what his home was like if he would choose to read here. "Let's walk up, shall we? The elevator's not very reliable." They started up the wide front stairwell, Simon in the lead. The semi-darkness was eerie and enchanting, with the statuary casting distorted shadows. She pushed down an impulse to put her hand in his. "Here we are." He pushed the button mechanism and held the door for her.

"Can you flip the switch on the right?" The hallway was suddenly illuminated, breaking the spell. "Just let me stop for the key to the vault." He darted into his office. How vast and frightening the building seemed. She knew the storage areas on the right held medieval weapons of torture, poison vials, and death masks intended for an upcoming sale. She shivered in spite of the heat, making a mental note not to return alone at night for any reason whatsoever. "Here we are." She jumped involuntarily as Simon returned.

They went farther down the corridor, saying nothing, until they reached the locked wire mesh door, which he opened. The looming irregular shapes, along with odd shafts of light from mirrors, gave the stacks the air of a surreal landscape, where grotesque figures might lurk. Stop that, she said to herself, or you'll never get to sleep tonight.

"Here it is." Simon opened the vault door and switched on the light. The chair sat on a sheet of canvas, molting fabric, and batting. Coils of discarded cording, in blue damask, hung down from it like tendrils. "Looks a little untidy, doesn't it?" Selena nodded solemnly, thinking of a little upholstery shop in Florence where the furniture in the window was always half-apart or half-together. Simon took her hand, leading her around to the chair's back. "Touch this." He guided her fingers into the wood frame.

"Ouch—it's rough!"

"Yes, of course it is. You see, it's been loved nearly to death."

"To death?"

"Yes. The interior wood—the frame—is so chewed up by the many reupholstering jobs that there's almost nothing left to tack any fabric onto. Oh, you didn't get a splinter, did you?" He took her hand and looked anxiously at her finger.

"No."

"Good. Well, then. Look at these legs." He reached down and caressed a hairy paw. "James Reynolds, the master carver of the Affleck shop, loved this wood. It's been worked with such tenderness and care and creativity. You can feel it. This chair was his *David*. Every ounce of his skill went into it. Here, give me your hand." He put Selena's hand under his. "Don't you feel him? We're touching him now, through all the years." She looked into his eyes, which were fevered and bright. His face had become intense and boyish. She wondered for an instant if he were mad, then decided she didn't care if he was.

"You do feel it, don't you? Oh, my darling girl!" He kissed her with such a tender sweetness that at first she didn't realize it was a kiss at all. It was more like being gathered up into the arms of a loving parent and surrounded with warmth, smothered with love. After the long, deep kiss, he pulled away, looking startled. She, unlike he, was completely composed.

"Of course I feel it, Simon. Of course I do."

Chapter 16

Freddie sat that hot July night on a peach damask *fauteuil* in his Bank Street apartment, cradling his head in his hands. Pancake make-up oozed onto his fingers. Tonight the music he listened to was not Debussy, but the turbulent, tortured strains of Scriabin's Etudes. It was after midnight, and Freddie, tired from the week at Bronte's and the enervating heat, couldn't think of sleep. Although he'd rouged his lips, put on his skin-tight jeans and the amulets, and tied a brilliant blue scarf around his neck, he knew that he would not go out. He never visited the Trucks in summer—the heat and the stench made them unbearable. He used to be able to walk Christopher Street, where a casual meeting might result in a fevered tryst. But that was before Duane. Since the evening of *Les Ballets Copacabana*, he could think of nothing else for himself, could want nothing else than to enfold the sweet young dancer in his arms.

What could he do? Duane wouldn't speak to him. He always got the answering machine with the same ridiculous message: "Hi, this is Dimitri. I'm auditioning right now (auditioning, indeed, Freddie thought), but you can call my manager, Wilhelm Dietz, at 288-5954." Click. Freddie had left ten messages in the last week alone. Duane hadn't answered any of them.

He got up, walked to the Regency mirror, and peered at himself with a critical eye. The reflection told him that he was slim, tall, acceptable-looking. He slowly unbuttoned his shirt. Body all right. A little flaccid from lack of exercise, a little hairless, as was his head. Damn the premature balding!

Was it that that bothered Duane? Why wouldn't he see him? Duane might have "engagements," and nights with men who were fat, repulsive and smelly. The thought of Duane with someone else horrified him, made him sick to his stomach. Perhaps if he could see him, he could win him over. Perhaps if Duane spent more time with him, he would come to care for him. If he could only reach him, *reason* with him. He turned from the mirror, walked to the silver tray holding crystal decanters, and poured himself a Courvoisier. As he swirled the amber liquid, he thought about a life with Duane. Duane here in his apartment, coming and going with his dancer's bag, scheduling auditions—real auditions—showering, singing, leaving dishes in the sink and socks on the floor. He wanted Duane more than he'd ever wanted anything, except his job at Bronte's. But Duane didn't want him—at least, not yet.

The glittering job used to be enough. He'd wanted it, gotten it. Somehow, he couldn't remember what had led him up to the heights in his work. He'd done exactly what he had to do to get to where he was. Mostly, he had flattered wealthy older women, and made himself an indispensably amusing escort and country houseguest. He'd studied hard, not only French antiques, but the mores and rituals of those who purchased them, and he had been an astute pupil. He'd made the proper friends with the proper pull at a place like Bronte's. His humor had always steered him through tricky political labyrinths. Then why? Why did none of his charm, or wit, or intelligence work with Duane?

The brandy and the swelling music were driving him mad. He had to do something. He had to get to Duane. And there was only one way.

He sat and looked at the telephone for a long time. The CD ended, and he didn't bother to change it, or to turn off the player, whose red digital lights seemed to stare at him like eyes saying, "Well? Well?"

He didn't have to look up the number. He knew it from the repeated hearings. Slowly, he pushed the buttons.

"Zis iss Wilhelm Dietz." The voice sounded foggy.

"Wilhelm, this is Freddie Trowbridge."

"*Bitte?*"

"Freddie Trowbridge. Olivier de Palance's business associate?"

" Ah, yes, viz ze hat. Vat do you vant?"

"I want to see Duane. Can you arrange it?" His stomach lurched.

"I am afraid Duane hass an audition on ze Vest Coast. He iss not in New York. May I suggest Robert? He vas in ze same corps as Duane, and his abilities as a dancer vill suit your needs just as vell."

How clever, Freddie thought. If Wilhelm were overheard, or if his wire was tapped, he'd sound just like a theatrical manager handling a booking.

"No, I'm afraid only Duane will do. When will he be back?" Freddie fought down the self-disgust he felt. He was speaking to scum, a pimp. He wanted to fling the phone against the wall, but he checked himself.

"He may not be back, Mr. Trowbridge. Who can tell?"

"What do you mean? Then you must tell me how to reach him."

"Zere iss no vay to reach him, Mr. Trowbridge."

"Look, Wilhelm. You know where he is. You must tell me. I'll pay. I'll pay anything." Freddie's voice was becoming louder, edged with hysteria. Wilhelm's response was an ugly laugh.

"It iss not a matter of money, Mr. Trowbridge." Did Freddie imagine the ironic accent on "Mister?" Or was he going crazy?

"I've got to find him! Tell me where he is, or I'll...."

"You vill vat? Don't ever threaten me, Mr. Trowbridge. People who threaten me are often...shall ve say, abruptly disconnected?"

"No, don't hang up, don't hang up. I'm sorry. It's only that...please, please tell me how to reach Duane."

"I am sorry. Duane does not vish to vork for you again—some little difficulty with the *tours-jetes*, I think he said?" Another nasty laugh punctuated the comment. Filth. Scum, Freddie thought. I could kill him.

"Stay avay from Duane, Mr. Trowbridge. He iss my special little boy. He says you haf been calling him. Try someone else. Now, Robert...."

"Never mind your Robert," Freddie spat into the phone. "And damn you to hell!" He flung the phone to the floor as if it scalded him. "Oh, my God, my God." He felt dizzy, sick. He was expert at suppressing anger, and seldom let the ugly chaos of it overwhelm him, but he was lost to it now.

He walked quickly up and down the room, moaning and gasping, trying to think. Duane didn't want him. Duane was on the Coast. Duane wouldn't see him. No, he didn't believe it, couldn't believe it. Hadn't Duane himself told him to call Wilhelm? And he had! It was Wilhelm's doing, it had to be. Wilhelm was keeping him from Duane for some sick reason of his own. How did Wilhelm know he'd been calling Duane unless Duane told him? And would Duane call from the Coast for that? Would it come up at all? If he were working, would he call his machine? Nothing made any sense, and Freddie sank into a chair and started the music again, turning up the volume as loud as it would go. The anguished strains of Scriabin masked the guttural sounds issuing from his throat.

He must find out. He must see Duane and straighten out this nightmare. It was the only way. He could discover whether or not Duane was in New York. He'd watch his room. He'd watched it before, many times. Then he'd know for sure whether the putrid words of Wilhelm were true.

Exhausted by his waning rage, he got up, turned down the music, and walked again to the mirror. Ghastly, just ghastly. The rouge had smeared, and his sparse hair was pasted in sweaty strings to his scalp and forehead, but there was no time for vanity. He knew he must get there to keep watch. It was well past midnight, and if Duane came home at all, it could be anytime between now and dawn. He'd wait across the street from Duane's window, like some craven, demented Romeo. He would wait as long as it took. Days, months—it didn't matter.

He ran out, leaving the lights burning. Once on the street, he went to 8th Avenue and hailed a taxi. The boogie-woogie of a Friday night in lower Manhattan was beating all around him, but he took no notice. He ordered the driver to take him to 43rd Street and 9th. On the trip, he prepared himself as well as he could for what he was about to do, to achieve.

When the cab let him off, he paid quickly, averting his face from the driver, went into a squalid bodega, and bought a can of lukewarm club soda. The brutality of the July heat was only beginning to subside at that hour, and his wait stretched out before him. It could be a long one. Long, and perhaps hopeless.

He stationed himself in a small, sheltered doorway across from Duane's room, careful not to disturb the sleeping derelict with whom he shared the space, and who, for all the world, looked to him like a heap of rags. His conscious mind pushed to ask him what he was doing, was he crazy? But he wouldn't allow those thoughts. He couldn't help himself, so why think about it? He took a long draught of the warm club soda. A thin rivulet of sweat ran down along his spine. The heap in the doorway stirred and mumbled.

The fetid odor set up by its motion caused Freddie to step out onto the sidewalk, but he didn't take his eyes from the small dark window across the street. The deep night in Hell's kitchen disgusted him, offended his sensibilities. It was ugly, it stank, it crawled with the verminous wreckage of humanity. He shuddered with revulsion. Why wouldn't Duane come to live with him? Why? Everything was so beautiful, so carefully arranged in his world. Why? He'd ask him.

Hours passed. He grew numb and groggy. The air was viscous with humidity. Passing vehicles spewed sulphurous fumes. He heard a sharp, small report: a gun? a car? By an act of superior will he rose above his senses and stayed rooted in the doorway, half-closed eyes still fixed on Duane's window.

When the light went on in the window, he thought he was hallucinating. Rubbing his eyes, he looked again. Two strong forearms were lifting the sash. With a sudden jump, he was out of the doorway. "*Duane, Duane,*" he called out, and ran across the street to the sidewalk below the window. The arms disappeared, and the sash closed with a crash.

"*No, No–Duane!* Let me in! I must speak to you. I *must.*" He began to bang in impotent frenzy on the ugly door between the Pink Pussycat Lounge and the souvenir shop. He voice became a wail, a lament, a screech. He banged repeatedly, until the door swung open and a huge man pushed at him hard.

"*Motherfucker!* I'm trying to get some sleep! Get *outta here,* or I'm gonna call the cops." He shoved Freddie roughly onto the sidewalk where he sank into a trembling heap. The door, opening onto a dingy hall, was slammed shut and locked. He was powerless to open it.

He sat on the pavement and tried to think, to plan, but he could only shiver in the heat of the July night. Thus preoccupied, he didn't notice the long black car slip up to the

140

curb by a fire hydrant, or the two men who emerged soundlessly, not bothering to click the doors shut. They advanced
on him with stunning speed. When Freddie looked up, a
heavy black rubber sap was already descending toward his
face. The first blow sent him sprawling full length on the
sidewalk, and he heard a sound like the breaking of a teacup. The other man, at the ready, struck at his genitals and
his kneecaps, while the first continued the volley of blows to
his head. He was too surprised to cry out. His left eye hurt
terribly, and he couldn't see out of it, but he thought it was
the wretched perspiration. He was thinking about how hot
it was when he slipped from consciousness, hearing one of
the men laughing, and the other muttering, "Compliments
of Wilhelm, fag. Next time, we'll...."

He awoke to see a rhythmical red light flashing and to
hear a siren wailing. He felt tired, terribly tired, but he
thought it was all right, that the two men in the green coats
would let him sleep there. They seemed nice. One was
saying to the other, "Don't touch the cuts. He may have it."
Freddie wondered idly what "it" was. He was a little worried.
He couldn't remember where he had left his hat.

※※※

"Selena...oh, Selena." The voice was a hoarse, cracked
whisper.

"Who is it? Anna? What's the matter?" Selena felt immediate alarm.

"He's dead, Selena. He's dead." Anna's voice broke off in
a husky sob, and Selena could hear only her labored
breathing.

"*Who's* dead? What are you talking about?"

"Walter Everest. He...he...shot...." Another sob.

"Anna, I can't understand you. Can you speak up?"

141

A strangled "No."

"Well, can you meet me? I'll get out for a few minutes."

"I'll try...yes...but not in the building, Selena. Not in the *building*." Anna's voice was rising in pitch, and Selena could detect the incipient hysteria in it.

"All right. Meet me at the front door in five minutes. We'll walk."

"Okay, Seely. We'll walk. Thanks. At the front door." Anna dropped the receiver.

Could it be true? Selena moved in double time, shaking off shock, trying to stay calm. What had Anna said? That Walter Everest was dead? It was horrible. But was she saying it was suicide? Or that he'd shot someone? For her, Anna's distress had been as shocking as the news she conveyed. Anna was so strong, so urban-wise, so knowing. Selena realized that she'd never seen her out of control before.

She grabbed her purse from the drawer and leaned around the partition to Arabella. "I have to go out for a few minutes. I'm sorry. Would you please answer my telephone?" Arabella nodded without looking up, and Selena bolted quickly down the hall and through the reception area. She used the time waiting for, and riding down on, the balky elevator to compose herself. The sense of unreality that descends when a tragedy or momentous event is underway was with her. Everything was changed; events were heightened, dulled, or pulled out of proper perspective.

She arrived first at the door. Nothing seemed unusual. James was ushering in clients, and the normal complement of limousines and chauffeured Mercedes' stood outside awaiting their riders' pleasure or whim. Then she saw Anna step off the elevator, looking as if she might be in shock. Her eyes stared wildly. There was an inappropriate smile on her face. She didn't seem to react to the stimulus of people and activity around her, but walked straight toward Selena, smiling that silly smile.

Don't let her collapse, Selena thought. Let her make it outside. As Anna neared her, Selena took her arm and rushed her through the double doors, nodding at James.

The burst of heat in the street seemed to slap at Anna, and Selena rushed her, half running, across the street, dodging traffic. Anna began to laugh wildly, and Selena took her shoulders and pushed her against the blank stone of a building's wall. The laughing soon became crying, and Selena let her weep until she tossed her head and said, "Okay...Seely...okay," and pushed Selena's hands away. Selena offered a small handkerchief, and Anna dabbed ineffectually at her eyes.

"Anna, what happened? What *is* it?"

"Walter Everest killed himself on Saturday."

"Oh, my God. How? Where?"

"In his office. He shot himself in the head with a dueling pistol."

"How horrible!"

"Yeah, it's horrible." Anna shuddered. "Let's walk, okay?" Selena nodded and fell into step.

"It's just that...*they* killed him, Selena. Wunnicke and his gang."

"Anna, no. They were unfair to him, but they didn't kill him. You mustn't think that."

"You don't know what's going on, Selena. *You don't know!*" Anna hissed.

"Then tell me," Selena said quietly. She felt helpless in the face of Anna's strong and inordinate emotion.

Anna began to talk fiercely. "We're putting out a press release right now to forestall any indelicate questions from the press, about how Mr. Everest 'accidentally' killed himself while cleaning a brace of antique dueling pistols, which, incidentally, will be included in a fall sale of antique firearms and weaponry. It wasn't an accident, Selena! They know it. But they're saying it was."

Selena nodded dumbly.

"He killed himself after the Saturday sale. They didn't find him until this morning. There was blood everywhere, they said, all over the desk and soaked into the carpet. And the walls!"

"Please, Anna, don't upset yourself any more over it. It happens on Wall Street, and in corporations, too, you know, and all over the world. People become despondent and just give up."

"But Selena, it's all so...ugly." They walked on in silence. Despite the daily dose of lurid newspaper stories, despite the violence all around them, the two friends hadn't really experienced violent death and its aftermath in their lives.

Anna said suddenly, "My grandfather died last year." Selena nodded. She understood instinctively the silent inventory Anna was making, the search for sense, for comparable experience and appropriate responses.

"Selena, I want to leave Endicott's—just walk out and never come back."

Selena was dismayed. "You can't, Anna! Think of yourself. Working at Endicott's will be important to you later. You want to be a bureau chief for Newsweek, right? And get in to Columbia Journalism? Please, please, don't leave now." She took Anna's arm and looked her in the eye, searching for a connection, for communication. Anna's troubled eyes stared back at her. "Don't leave *me!* I'll miss you too much."

Anna sighed heavily. "It's not just Walter Everest, you know. It's other things, too. Terrible things." In spite of the heat, Anna shivered. "Let's go in to this deli."

Pungent smells, the hum of refrigeration equipment and the sounds of someone sweeping in a back room greeted them. Selena realized how hot she was.

"What'll you have, girlies?" A short, smiling Latino man presided over a counter full of meats, cheeses, and other delectables.

"Two diet Cokes." Anna looked at Selena, who nodded confirmation.

"Is that *all?*"

"No, of *course* not. I just want to order one thing at a time, every fifteen minutes or so."

The man eyed Anna sharply, then broke into a laugh and fetched the Cokes. Anna cast her eyes skyward. Selena was relieved at her friends' burst of sarcasm; it seemed, well, normal. This was the Anna she knew, the real Anna. They moved to one of the two tiny tables in the front of the deli, and sat down. Anna put her two fists to her eyes, and leaned heavily on the table, Selena watching her closely. They took long, thirsty drafts of the sweet liquid. Selena waited for Anna to speak.

"Endicott's is full of rot and maggots."

"Is it?"

"The press office makes me sick, Seely. Alex Putnam is a complete cokehead. He's high almost all the time. Diana covers for him, but it's *so* obvious. And he goes to all the elegant receptions and deals with the press like he's Prince Charles or something."

"That sort of situation usually resolves itself in the end."

"Yes, but when's the end? Selena, think about it! When's the end?"

Selena simply shrugged.

"He screws boys in his office."

"What?"

"You heard me. I've worked late, and I see them go in, and the door closes, and there's laughing and pounding and banging and grunting...."

"Oh, Anna, are you sure?"

"Positive. Sid told me he's been had on a Louis XV desk."

A fleeting image of a pretty boy intern—Sidney—crossed before Selena's eyes.

They sipped at their Cokes, and Selena thought about how to respond to her friend's disclosures. "Well, that's disgusting, but it doesn't affect you. At least *you're* not being pinioned to desks, or anything."

"I told you, you have the only normal boss in the place. Oh! I totally forgot! How was your date?"

"It was fine. I'll tell you about it later." A sudden memory of a touch, a kiss, a dark night of mysterious implications in the place of "rot and maggots" overcame her.

"Anna, I know you're upset. You've every right to be. Telling lies for the greater good of Endicott's can't possibly make you happy, especially since you're such a good journalist. But please, please, think of yourself. You can't bring Walter Everest back. You can't reform Alex Putnam. You're only a summer intern. You're not committed to Endicott's. But if you make enemies, or a poor showing, it will hurt you forever."

"You really believe that, don't you, Selena? You believe in letting them win?"

"How can you say that? Of *course* not. I just don't believe in letting them make you lose."

Anna slurped the last drops of her soda, and banged the can down. "There's more. I just don't know if I can stand to tell you now."

"Why not? It can't be worse than suicide, drug addiction, and sodomy, can it?"

"Well, it isn't as disgusting, perhaps, but it is much more serious for the company."

"So...tell me!"

"Sarah Dean and Wunnicke are cheating our consignors."

146

"How?"

Anna went through the details of the policy of lying to consignors of items that didn't reach their reserve amount, in order to get them to accept a lower bid.

"That's unethical! But why are they doing it? The money can't be that important to Endicott's bottom line."

"Every little bit is important to people like them. There are no limits on greed." Then, lowering her voice, she said, "It's more than unethical, Selena. Part of what they are doing is illegal. I've heard that when they think they can get away with it, they offer a consignor less than the actual amount bid. They pad the reserve, which means that Endicott's gets an extra profit—but it's money that rightfully should go to the consignor."

"Oh, Anna! Are you certain? But this is terrible! Endicott's most valuable asset is the trust it has earned over the years. If those two are cheating clients, stealing from them...." She thought for a moment, and then asked, "How many people know about this?"

"Too many, I suspect. I think every department head is involved—with the basic program, anyway; I doubt that many of them know about the reserve padding—and every one has been told to comply. That includes Mr. Simon Haden-Jones. I'm surprised that you haven't been asked to participate, asked to do some of the telephoning with the other interns."

"Simon would never agree to something so despicable!" Selena was irate. "He's too honorable."

"Well, apparently everybody else has agreed, because it's happening."

Selena was stunned by the revelation. Standing up to go, she staggered, feeling sickened by the heat and the emotional intensity of the exchange with Anna. She grasped the table edge to steady herself.

"I don't believe it, Anna. I can't."

"Believe it, Seely. Endicott's is a place where people die—one way or another."

The young women walked back into the hot sunshine and noise. Selena couldn't think. Nothing seemed to make sense, or to matter. She was deeply affected by Anna's litany. As they reached Endicott's front doors, Anna said, "I'm so sorry, Selena. The world is ugly, even in here. Maybe we'll remember this as the summer when all our illusions were shattered forever. About the illegal reserve policy: ask Arabella. You'll find out."

Selena nodded, and bit her lip to keep from crying in the cramped elevator. It wouldn't do to upset the lady in the purple straw hat, crooning to the poodle in her arms.

Chapter 17

Simon approached the entrance to St. Luke's-Roosevelt Hospital Center with dread. He had been horrified to receive a call that Freddie had been mugged, and surprised that it came from an intern and not from Freddie himself. Unpleasantness always bothered him, but this was unthinkable. The city's underside was seeping into his carefully ordered world, and he didn't like it. He would have to deal with some gruesome details, but his concern for Freddie propelled him forward. He hoped devoutly that Freddie wasn't seriously hurt. Robberies and attacks were becoming increasingly violent in New York, and the injuries sustained by victims were becoming worse—often far worse.

At the fourth floor desk he asked a nurse for Mr. Trowbridge's room.

"Let's see—417. Oh, don't let him talk much."

A shiver of revulsion ran through him. "Why not? Is he badly hurt?"

"The doctor will speak to you about that. You are a relative?"

"Yes," Simon lied without hesitation, and started down the corridor.

The door to room 417 was open. He took a deep breath, willing himself to smile no matter what, and strode in with a confidence he did not feel. The sight in the bed stopped him cold. Freddie's face was a mass of purple. One eye was swollen shut, and he had to use a bar suspended across the bed to raise and lower himself. Simon let out a gasp. "My God, Freddie, what happened?"

"Hello...*mon ami.*" Freddie managed a half smile on the good side of his face. "Good to see you." He seemed exhausted and barely able to speak.

"Don't tire yourself. Don't talk if it hurts. Is there anything I can get for you? Anything you need?" Simon sat gingerly on the one visitor's chair.

Freddie shook his head no.

"Were you robbed? Who was it? What did he want?"

Freddie shrugged his shoulders. "Two hairy apes...jumped out of a car...and beat the hell...out of me." He shifted in the bed, and Simon saw the tubes running out of his arm. Noticing Simon's stare, Freddie said, "It's my...cheekbone... you see. They...shattered it. Looks like...*merde*...but it will heal soon. I'll be...out of here...in no time."

"I hope so, sport. This is no fun."

"Oh, *au contraire*...it is, it is...*copain.* Healthful...food... served in bed...maid service...a veritable spa." Again, the contorted half-smile. There was a pregnant silence, and Simon squirmed uncomfortably on the too-small chair.

"Could I get you some books? Or magazines?" Simon wasn't good at giving comfort, and he knew it and felt helpless. To his great relief, Freddie nodded.

"Would you get me...the new *Antiques*? And...*Connaissance des Arts*?"

"Of course. I'll have the press office send them over to you this afternoon."

"*Merci* and...thanks. Thank you...for coming."

The nurse appeared at the door and motioned to Simon that the visit should end.

"Well, I've got to get back. The catalogs are about to go to press, and you know what that's like." Freddie nodded and held up an arm.

"Would you please call...Christian...for me? Explain. Tell him I'll be back...in no time...and that...Danielle can...hold the...ramparts."

"I will. Don't worry."

Freddie's good eye closed and he shifted in the bed, grimacing in pain. Simon looked away.

"Goodbye, sport. See you on the outside."

A weak "cheery-bye" came from the bed. Simon rose and walked quickly down the hall, hating the hospital smells, and deeply troubled by Freddie's injuries and the odd circumstances he'd described. Two men jumping out of a car and beating him without the motive of robbery? It didn't make much sense unless.... He realized then that the beating must have had to do with Freddie's homosexuality. It was something he could never ask about, and would never know. Nor did he wish to.

Back on 76th street, he gulped the exhaust-fouled air to expunge the smells of the hospital. He was shaken by seeing Freddie incapacitated, but the incident no longer seemed a random violence. What had Freddie done? Who had beaten him? He willed himself not to think about it. He couldn't afford the time, now; he was much too busy. He'd send the magazines. He'd call him from time to time. Freddie would soon recover, and he could forget all about it.

By the time he reached Endicott's, he was perspiring profusely. The ride in the elevator was more vexing than usual, and he couldn't wait to break free of it and the others in it. Once inside his cool, dark office, he breathed a sigh, sat down, picked up the phone, and pushed the two digits for an Endicott's extension. "Alex, please. It's Haden-Jones."

"One minute, Mr. Haden-Jones."

The next voice he heard was not Alex's, but Diana's. "May I help you? Alex is tied up just now."

"Can you please send by messenger the latest copies of *Antiques* and *Connaissance des Arts* to Freddie Trowbridge at St. Luke's-Roosevelt Hospital, room...one moment...417?"

151

"Is this official Endicott's business, Mr. Haden-Jones?"

"Bill my department, damn it. And thank you." Simon couldn't afford to be annoyed by the petty bookkeeping standards Wunnicke had mandated. He didn't want to call Christian Thomas, head of Bronte's, but he had to. Freddie had no family except for distant cousins—at least, that's what he'd always told Simon—so whom else could he ask for a favor? Simon sighed, pushed the buttons, and started fiddling with his quill pen, tickling himself by drawing it back and forth under his chin.

The switchboard operator answered, "Bronte's."

"Christian Thomas, please." He was put on hold.

"Mr. Thomas' office." Simon repeated his name. "It's urgent."

"Mr. Thomas is in a meeting, Mr. Haden-Jones. I'll see if I can put you through." After a few moments, a very cultivated British voice came over the wire.

"Hello, Simon. What can I do for you?"

"Christian, I'm sorry to intrude, but I've just come from St. Luke's Hospital, and I was asked by Freddie Trowbridge to tell you that he'd been mugged early Saturday morning. Evidently he was in intensive care over the weekend, and I was called only this morning.

"Yes, I see."

"His injuries look rather bad to me. His face is livid, but he says he'll be back soon, and that his assistant, Danielle, can carry on if you'll speak to her."

"Ummmm. Yes."

"Perhaps you'll want to call him in a day or two?"

"That won't be necessary."

"Oh?" Simon was surprised at the emotionless calm with which Christian was taking the news, which was understated even for a Brit.

"Simon, you may as well know. We've already heard about

Freddie. I was called at home on Sunday by Maxine Garrett, that scurrilous gossip-monger from the *New York Post*. It seems they had someone stationed at St. Luke's Hospital's emergency room over the weekend to watch for possible embarrassing situations for the Upper East Side society set. Unfortunately, he recognized Freddie. Or rather, he heard the name given by the two ER interns who brought him in."

"What difference does that make?" Simon remembered his own treatment at the hands of the editors of the *Post* when his son was killed. He'd never forgotten, nor forgiven.

"It seems they've done a little investigating, and they have uncovered more than a simple mugging. According to Ms. Garrett, Freddie is implicated in some unsavory homosexual business."

"That's rot, Christian. They can't print garbage like that."

"That is precisely what we're waiting to see. Ms. Garrett says she's going to break the story shortly, and wants a 'comment' from me. Of course, I won't give one."

"What 'story' does she say she has?"

"We'll have to wait and see if the woman is bluffing, Simon, and how damaging the information may be. We're very harsh on scandal here at Bronte's, particularly the homosexual kind. The powers-that-be in England simply won't stand for it."

Simon shook his head in disgust. "Thank you for telling me, Christian. I won't say anything to Freddie. He's not in any condition to be worried on that score."

"It may turn out to be nothing at all. Most of their stories are pure helium."

"I devoutly hope so."

"Thank you for calling, Simon. May I offer a word of caution? Should this story turn out to be true, I'd consider, well, disassociating myself from Mr. Trowbridge. At once."

Simon's pulse sped; he felt cold; he couldn't speak.

Finally, he managed. "Yes. Thank you. Goodbye."

What was happening? He wondered whose goddamn business it was *what* Freddie did when he was off-duty. He had been an asset to Bronte's for over twelve years. They had loved his ability to garner publicity for them, to court the wealthy widows and minor royals. Was he now facing ostracism, oblivion? What would Bronte's do to him? Where was loyalty, anyway? Indeed, where was it at Endicott's?

Simon felt a deep hollow from his throat to his stomach, and an aching sickness welling up. He remembered the awful feeling, which he'd experienced only twice before: once, when he knew, finally and without a doubt, that his father's illness had been hidden from him until it was too late; and when he knew with certainty that his wife was having an affair. It was a feeling unlike any other, a betrayal that clasped him like an ugly parasite, that wouldn't let go, that made him ill, that made him think of murder—or suicide—and that made him certain that a life which could contain such misery was not worth living.

He had found the strength to go on those other times. Could he find it now? He put down his pen and sat very still, the weight on his chest making it almost impossible to breathe, the dull pain settling somewhere near his heart.

Chapter 18

"Simon?" The door to his office opened slightly, and he saw Selena's face looking at him questioningly. "I knocked twice." She looked hesitant.

He stirred, tipped forward toward the desk. "Come in, Selena. Please come in."

She settled herself across from him and gave him a worried glance. "Simon, I don't know how to feel about Mr. Everest's suicide." He was completely taken aback, not realizing that the interns—his intern—would be affected by the recent violence within the walls of the citadel.

"None of us does, Selena. It's terrible." He looked at her with compassion. Poor girl. She's too young, too unseasoned to deal with suicide. All of his protective instincts were stirred. He wanted to hold her, comfort her. Instead, he cleared his throat. "Please don't worry. Walter was a troubled man, not able to cope."

"Then you think that Endicott's had nothing to do with it?"

"Endicott's? Well, yes it had something to do with it, of course, but people react to adversity in very different ways. Walter Everest chose the one he chose."

Looking at her shoes, she said, "Suicide." Then there was a silence. The word lay in the air between them.

When she spoke again, it was about a different subject, one that distressed her even more, and was the real reason for her visit. "I'd like to know about the new reserve policy."

He was stunned. The look she gave him was full of troubled intensity. It made him uncomfortable. He shifted in his chair and averted his gaze, then cleared his throat twice, but said nothing.

"Then you did know about it?" Her voice was almost a whisper.

"Selena, yes, I knew. But I never agreed to it for this department. Never for a moment."

"I see." She stood up abruptly. "Thank you for telling me."

"Don't you see? It's just a cheap, short-term scheme that Miss Dean has instituted to impress Mr. Wunnicke. It will die a natural death, and American Furniture will never be party to it. Never."

She shot him an agonized glance. "But Simon. It's all so...so *wrong!*"

He took a deep breath. "Of course it's wrong. But you'll find...as you grow older and go out into the world...nothing is ever perfect...or black and white." He stood up and reached out to touch her shoulder, but she shrank from him in anticipation of the gesture.

"Excuse me. I have things to do." She turned abruptly and left the office.

Oh, God, Simon thought, oh, God. What is happening here? Why is this happening to me? I've got a department to run. I'm an important figure in my profession. I can't disable myself because my best friend is in an ugly mess and my love thinks I'm unprincipled. For God's sake! He returned crossly to his papers, but somehow couldn't convince himself he was important in any way.

Selena sat down heavily at her crowded desk and felt hot tears welling up in her eyes. All right, so he knew. He's not perfect after all. But he's not one of them. Is he? I should have known. Just because he's a bit older, he's not my father. Did I want him to be? Suddenly, she knew that she had to talk to her father, had to tell him what was occurring.

He would know how to interpret the dishonesty of the reserve policy, and how to put the suicide in perspective. She was sure he'd know. She glanced at the clock: 11:30. She could go home at lunch and maybe catch him at cocktails. She sat miserably, shuffling papers she was supposed to be filing, somehow unable to look at them or see them clearly. Please, please, let him be there!

She waited in tense passivity until 12:30, then grabbed her purse and ran down the long corridor, through reception, down the stairs past the Brancusi sculpture, out into the harsh heat and sunlight of Park Avenue. She sprinted up the street, dodging the strolling lunch crowd and delivery bicycles and elderly ladies arm in arm, running through swerving cars and taxis and strollers, until she reached her building. She ran up the steps, impatiently inserted her key, and took the interior steps two at a time. She fumbled with the keys, let herself into the apartment, and dived for the air conditioner, turning it on high and putting her face squarely in front of the tepid blast of air that came forth. She was so out of breath she could only gasp, and after a moment, went to the kitchen and took a bottle of cold water from the refrigerator, gulped it thirstily, and then sprinkled some on her face with two fingers.

How will I put all this to Papa? What do I want him to know? Do I want help, or advice, or just what? She knew enough to organize her thoughts, and decided to leave out the part about her budding romance with Simon. That was all too complicated, and her feelings were too young and unformed. There hadn't been enough time together to test them. She leaned back against the wall, rolling the bottle around on her forehead. She had thought about him a great deal. She had daydreamed about lying next to him, holding

157

him and letting him kiss her with that sweet, enveloping kiss, and falling into the warmth of him, but it hadn't happened yet, except in her imagination. No, she couldn't speak of it.

Regaining some composure, she sat on the futon and pushed the buttons of the phone, marveling at the rapidity of the connection.

"Villa Fraccese." It was the voice of a housemaid.

"*Signore Fraccese, por favore. Questa e su figlia.*"

"*Uno momento.*" After a short wait, she heard his voice.

"*Selena, dove se? Stai bene?*"

"*Si, si,* Papa. I'm...at home for lunch, that's all."

"*Bene.* That's fine. Then, hello."

"Oh, Papa! There are such bad things going on at Endicott's. I don't know what to do."

"What things, *cara?*"

"They're cheating consignors with a secret reserve policy, Papa! And they're making everyone a party to it...or else."

"Or else what?"

"They'll be fired."

"I see." After a silence, her father said. "Is this what's bothering you?"

"Not all of it. The company president committed suicide because they were forcing him out, Papa. They broke his contract and they weren't going to give him anything. He was disgraced."

"Yes, we read about that. But this is not the way the newspapers reported it."

"But that's another part of it! They made the press office lie about it all! My friend told me all about it!

"I'm sorry to hear this. But who is 'they'?"

"The owner and his executives. Papa, what shall I do?"

"I don't know, *cara.* Do you want to come home?"

She thought of Simon, and Anna, and Julio and Loretta,

and the glamorous receptions at Endicott's. "No...no. What would that solve? Of course not! Not unless I have to. I...I guess I want to make things right."

"Can you do this? Can you make any difference there?"

"I don't know, Papa. I don't know."

"This is what you must do when you see something wrong. You must ask yourself, 'Can I make it right? Can I even begin to make it right?'"

"Yes, I must. But I don't know what I can do, Papa. I'm just an intern."

"Think about it, Selena. Then decide. Remember: You can always come home. We're lonely for your pretty face."

"Thank you, darling Papa. I'll think about it. I'll let you know."

"Selena?"

"Yes, Papa?"

"Don't do anything foolish. But don't be miserable about things you can't change. Sometimes you must walk away."

"Thank you, Papa. I'll think for a while. Give my love to Mama."

"I will, *cara*. Call again soon, *si?*"

"Of course I will. *Arrivederci*, Papa." She put the phone down slowly. Was there anything she could do, apart from feeling this way or that about it? That was the crux of the matter, and her father had put it all into focus in three minutes.

)O(O(

"Now listen *up!*" Julio clapped his hands together in an unmistakable command, and the whispering and giggles coming from the crowd in Selena's apartment ceased. He looked around at the dozen or so assembled young people with a stern glare. "Selena's going to talk to us about why

159

we're going to picket." Selena stood up and a low wolf whistle emanated from the back of the room. Julio glowered vaguely in the direction of the sound while Selena smiled hesitantly.

"As Julio has told you, the demonstration will be on Saturday, August 29, all day, in front of Endicott's, at Park Avenue and 63rd. We'll need a lot of big banners and signs, done up in primary colors: red, blue...."

"I do *great* signs, man." A handsome black youth stood up to a ripple of applause. "You should see my graffiti on the post office."

"Sit *down*, Lorenzo, I'm not kidding! This is for real," Julio warned.

"Endicott's has been committing some illegal and terrible practices, and it's time they were exposed," Selena said.

"But don't you guys work there?" A girl with enormous clanking earrings nodded at her, Anna, and Sidney.

"Yes, we do. We're summer interns—which is why we cannot be connected with this demonstration in any way. If you see us, please pretend not to know us."

"But I don't get it. Why are you doing this picketing thing if you work there?" Lorenzo asked.

"Because we believe in Endicott's, but we *don't* believe in some of the bad people there, or in what they are doing. Their clients deserve much better—and so do we," Selena answered. There were some murmurs and a few shrugged shoulders.

"So what do you want the signs to say?" Lorenzo asked. Anna stood up at this question.

"I've made a list. Let's see—the first is 'ENDICOTT'S UNFAIR TERMINATION POLICY.'"

"Termination?"

"Firing—you know."

"Oh, yeah. How do you spell that?"

"I've written it down," Anna continued. "'ENDICOTT'S PADS RESERVES.'"

"Check."

"And 'SEXUAL HARASSMENT AT ENDICOTT'S.'" Anna finished dramatically. Sid blushed and coughed.

Selena spoke again. "We cannot thank you enough for helping us. We'd do it ourselves, but the politics are just too complicated. Anna will see to it that all the press and TV stations are there, so do look your best."

"That's okay, Selena. Beats picketing the welfare department for the rights of single mothers." Lorenzo smiled, showing brilliant white teeth.

Loretta, who had been conferring with Julio, spoke up. "I've made a schedule of who marches from what time to what time. Julio will take care of the permits. We'll have the signs in the Shecky's Pizza van, and Julio will park around the corner between deliveries—also to change shifts. You know, that little dead end street? There will also be free pizza and cokes for every picketer." A chorus of "yays" and "all rights" followed her announcement. Julio rose again.

"Okay, has everybody got what they're supposed to do?" There was a light flutter of assent. "See you next Saturday."

The colorfully dressed young people began to file out of the apartment. Selena stood at the door, smiling and thanking them. Lorenzo stayed the longest, conferring with Anna about the picket signs.

"I feel rather sick," Sid, pale as a vapor, said as he leaned against the doorway to the kitchen.

"Don't worry, Sid. You'll never be connected to this demonstration. And you're doing something to be proud of. Alex Putnam won't be able to seduce next summer's interns quite so prodigally."

"Well, it wasn't really so awf...."

"Sidney!"

161

"All right. Call me if you need me for anything else—preferably in the dead of night."

"Just remember—you're not just doing a good thing—you're doing the *right* thing," Anna said. Sid nodded and walked unsteadily to the door, colliding with Lorenzo, who gave him a toothy grin.

Anna and Selena looked at each other.

"Well, Seels, we're doing it."

"Yes, we are, Anna." They moved to the futon and sat down, clearing away some plastic cups and napkins. "Will it work?"

"You're damned right it will work!" Anna's face was intense and twisted. "The demonstration alone certainly will embarrass Mr. Wunnicke and Ms. Dean. And it'll get the media out. Then we can leak the story to the *Times*. Some reporter there will be smart enough to follow it up. We'll get them, Selena. We'll get them. It feels so good to be doing it, doesn't it? Doesn't it?"

They looked at each other again, and clasped hands, holding on to each other tightly with a mixture of excitement and fear.

XOXOX

"Well, it's just *too* ridiculous, you know. They are taking mysterious cues from *The National Enquirer* or some other rag." Freddie moved the phone from one ear to the other, avoiding his swollen cheek, and relaxed onto his sofa. "Not a word, of *course* not. What? No...no. Just taking a little time off to regrow my skeletal structure and return to my previous sartorial splendor. Fired? Fired? Of course not, old thing! How really lunatic! Bronte's can't do without me. Christian told me himself. Yes—I'll be fit as a flute, *mon ami*, and back to work in no time. Lovely of you to call...*a tout a*

162

l'heure...cheery-bye." Freddie's voice broke before the last words were out.

Trying to hang up the phone, he missed the cradle, and the elegant handset fell downward, where it lolled at the end of the cord until he was roused from his trancelike state by the clicking and eventual "Please hang up" emanating from it. Wearily he replaced the receiver, and his eye caught the letter lying on the table before him, its ends curling upward from the folds. He looked at it sideways, afraid to acknowledge it, thinking of it as a piece of dangerous, deadly, polluted matter. Radioactive, perhaps. Extraterrestrial clay sent to destroy all who came near it

But in the end it was only a letter. Not even a personal one, but one that a computer had printed out, changing only the name of the addressee and his years of service. He poked at it with his forefinger until the top two-thirds was visible. It read:

August 17, 1987

Dear Mr. Trowbridge:

As we have discussed, your employment with Bronte's will be terminated today. You are entitled to severance pay computed by the ratio of one week's salary for each year's service. You have completed 13.2 years of service this month. You may expect to receive your final check within one week.

Your 401K plan may be distributed to you in a lump sum, or rolled over into another approved plan within six months. For lump sum distribution, your beneficiary must sign a waiver of survivor annuity. For questions relating to continuance of your health insurance, please contact Frances Knightley in human resources.

We wish you every success in your future endeavors.

Sincerely,

The signer's name wasn't visible until he unfolded the rest of the missive.

"*Who* discussed it, old things? Just who? *I* wasn't there!"

The only indication that there was any human choice involved in the process was three words, scrawled at the bottom in Christian Thomas' flowing script: "I'm so sorry."

Freddie threw his head back, causing his cheek to throb. The words danced in the neon dark behind his eyelids. I'm so sorry. I'm so sorry. So sorry I couldn't even tell you, but had to send a fatal letter, a declaration of my cowardice.

Not so sorry as I am, Christian. Not nearly so sorry.

It had been only two days since the *New York Post* had broken its odious story as part of a new series entitled "Gay Bashing in New York." What a plum for Maxine Garrett, to find someone with Freddie's connections in society to expose. Freddie guessed that the circulation of the *Post* had leaped that day. The headline was irresistible: DAPPER BRONTE'S EXPERT BEATEN IN HOMO-SEXSCANDAL.

The second lead read: "Post Exposes Male Prostitution Ring." The article was illustrated with a full length picture of him in his bowler, resting on a cane in front of Bronte's, with insets of headshots of Wilhelm and Duane. He scanned the opening lines for the hundredth time: "Freddie Trowbridge, well-known French furniture expert at Bronte's, a premier art auction house, was brutally beaten by thugs protecting a lucrative prostitution ring using boy dancers...." At the article's end, Ms. Garrett promised further titillation: "Next week: The leather mask murders."

It was all so sordid! What did this yellow journalism do, he wondered, but sell a few papers and ruin a few lives? It was the sort of mindless destructiveness he hated most. He had never felt so sickened.

He sighed and touched his bruised cheekbone tenderly. There was only one immediate consolation: drink. And he definitely was going to console himself. He had carefully collected a small "cellar" of fine wines and cognacs, and had been known to joke that when the time came to "leave the stage," he would simply imbibe himself to death. At Roberto's loft, in the days when he'd been playing the life-and-death game, he'd say, "No ghastly lesions for me, boys. I'll drown in my own little ocean of Chateau Lafitte Rothschild, *merci.*"

He moved painfully to the refrigerated cave he'd created in the rear of his kitchen, selected a Chateau Margaux 1933, uncorked it, and poured the deep red liquid into a beautiful cut-crystal glass. He drank until the bottle was empty. Then he opened a bottle of Reims champagne, selected a tulip glass, and drank it down without stopping. When he could no longer taste the exquisite wines, he poured a snifter of Courvoisier.

What did I do? he thought. What did I do? I only loved a boy. I never hurt him. I only wanted to help him and love him and have him love me back. He took another draft of the cognac, letting it warm his throat.

But he didn't. And now it's over. It's all over. He set the snifter down. "Why isn't this working?" he said aloud.

He moved unsteadily to his desk and took out a sheet of writing paper and a pen. His brain was reeling and his hand unsteady, but he wrote. A few lines, only four. Then he folded the paper, lopsided, and tucked it awkwardly into an envelope, which he sealed. On the envelope he wrote "To: Simon Haden-Jones".

When he stood up, he felt the room swirl, but he walked haltingly to the mirror, tripping on a corner of the rug and banging his wrist against a table. He didn't notice the stab of pain.

"Old man, you look a mess," he said out loud, and ran his fingers through his sparse hair. He stumbled unsteadily down the hall toward the bedroom. Switching on the *bouillotte* lamp, he opened a drawer of his *semanier* and pawed clumsily through it until he found his shirt studs, eyeing them closely to be sure they were the correct ones for summer. He lunged for the door of the closet, reached inside for his white dinner jacket, a red polka dot bow tie and cummerbund, and his new white straw boater.

"Dressing well is the best revenge," he slurred, hopping on one leg and trying to insert the other into a white linen trouser leg. In his blurred vision, the room began to dance. He quite liked the idea, and began humming a little French tune, "*Ne me quittes pas*," addressing it to the jacket, the shirt, the tie, and the hat, which he finally put onto his head after three unsuccessful attempts.

When he had completed his habiliments, he walked as erectly as his drunken state would allow into the living room and stared at the reflection in the mirror.

"Ta Da! *Mon Dieu*, I am *soigné!* He gave himself a loopy grin and touched the brim of his hat in a debonair salute. Then he walked back to the kitchen, caught up the bottle of cognac and the exquisite snifter that the Duchess d'Arbres had given him, loving the feel of it in his hand, and walked carefully toward the apartment's front door. He flung it open and walked with great dignity of carriage down the hall to the tiny elevator. As he waited, he began to sing "*Je ne regrette rien*," and suddenly a gasp caught at his throat. "Poor little sparrow!" he sobbed. When the elevator arrived, he was nearly in tears, and when he entered it and pushed the button marked "R" for roof, he was thinking only of Piaf, the little sparrow.

166

Chapter 19

"Haden-Jones?—Martin Wunnicke." Simon was surprised to hear Wunnicke's voice on the telephone. He was enjoying his first Saturday puttering around in his apartment in the lull before the fall auction frenzy, and was nonplussed by the unexpected interruption.

"Yes, sir?"

"We've got some goddamn riffraff walking around on the sidewalk with some signs on poles."

"Are you at Endicott's?"

"Of *course* I'm at Endicott's. They're not picketing my apartment, for chrissakes."

Simon sighed. He had been sipping coffee and chortling over the hyperbole in the proofs of the *House & Garden* article on his apartment. When the phone rang, he had been laughing with delight at the purple prose of Letitia Granby in describing his use of a pair of ancient lances as drapery rods: "The learned Mr. Haden-Jones draws upon the deepest recesses of his ancestral memory, transforming the noble weapons into the shields of his fenestrations." Just like her, the knee-grabbing wench.

"Haden-Jones?"

"Yes, Mr. Wunnicke. How can I help?" He snapped back to the reality of the voice on the phone.

"We don't know what the hell this is about. Can you come on over?" Simon sighed again.

"I'll be there in forty minutes." He put down the phone and drained the coffee, savoring the last drops. As he shaved and showered, the information Wunnicke had conveyed so tersely sank in. Pickets? he thought. There hasn't been any union trouble at Endicott's. The movers and truckers are happy. So are the cleaning staff and the security guards. He wondered idly what it was all about as he slipped into khaki slacks, loafers, and a blue polo shirt. He slicked his damp hair back from his forehead. As he walked from his lobby into the quiet street, it struck him that it was odd for Martin Wunnicke to be at Endicott's on a Saturday in the heat of August. There were no sales, there was no reason for him to be there. He decided that, no matter what, nothing would spoil his day—not Wunnicke, not some picketers, nothing. He had two tickets in his pocket for The Royal Shakespeare Company's production of *Les Liaisons Dangereuses* for that evening, and he was taking Selena. The thought of holding her hand during the performance made him giddy, and he remembered the other hot summer night's evening with her with a frisson of delight.

Nothing could have prepared him for what saw as he turned the corner onto Park Avenue. This demonstration was no quiet picketing by disgruntled employees. The scene before him was a mad urban mural of colors and tints. The demonstrators were kids, mostly black and Hispanic, dressed in cut-offs, T-shirts and wildly colored baseball caps. One youth was on the sidewalk, twirling madly upon one shoulder, his legs crisscrossing rhythmically in the air to the low pulse of a huge boom box sitting next to him at ear level. A mistake, Simon's first impulse told him. They can't have anything to do with Endicott's. It's a bloody mistake! Then he saw the signs.

Huge, rectangular signs, gaily colored, were mounted on long poles carried aloft. As he hurried closer, he read "Endicott's Unfair Termination Policy". The sign furthest from him was carried by a slight girl, and as she turned he read "Sexual Harassment at Endicott's."

168

He flushed with a very real anger, and stonily pushed his way through the noisy, milling demonstrators, and through Endicott's elegant double doors. How dare they? He felt no interest whatsoever in the cause these people were dramatizing in such a public fashion, if indeed there was a cause. Again, something ugly and unruly was seeping into his world, and he wanted to shake it off, put it from him. Al, the security guard, walked up to him. "Hello, Mr. Haden-Jones. Some business, huh?"

"How long have they been here?"

"Since 10 o'clock, sir. Miss Dean was here, and she called Mr. Wunnicke and the police right away."

"Did the police come?"

"Oh, yes, sir. Said they couldn't do anything. These kids have a permit of some sort."

"A permit?" Hang it all, this was insane. He watched the motley parade through the plate glass window.

"Yessir. And Mr. Wunnicke's hopping mad."

"I'm sure he is, Al. Keep an eye on this, will you?"

Al responded by patting the pistol on his hip. Oh, God, Simon thought.

He took the stairs two at a time, and jogged to the second floor executive offices, where he could see Wunnicke, Sarah Dean, and an exhausted-looking Harris Tompkins in animated conversation. Wunnicke motioned Simon in.

"What the *hell* is this, Simon? We can't have this!"

"I truly don't know, sir. I can't understand it." Sarah shot him a glance of veiled dislike.

"Did you *see* those signs? Kids like that don't make that kind of sign." A vein bulged in Wunnicke's temple, and he began to pace back and forth. Sarah spoke.

"Martin, I think it has something to do with Walter Everest's suicide. Maybe his family put them up to it."

"Maybe, Sarah, but didn't you see those other goddamn

169

signs?" He resumed his pacing. Simon was deeply disturbed and extremely uncomfortable in the presence of these three—"the enemy," as he thought of management.

"What'd those damn signs say, Harris?"

Tompkins answered wearily, "One of them says 'Sexual Harassment at Endicott's.'"

"What the *hell* is that? We don't have any sexual harassment here. *My god.* There're women all over the place." No one could answer the apparent non sequitur.

Finally, Harris spoke laconically, "Actually, most of our male employees wouldn't bother women, and...."

"Oh, shut up, Harris." Wunnicke glared at him.

Sarah smiled a little, and said, "We probably should have named a new president right away, as soon as Walter died, to handle all of this." She thought: I'm tired of waiting, Martin; if I had the reins, I'd handle this little demonstration just fine. Don't you see what your delay is costing you? She looked at him pointedly.

"Well, we've got to get them out of here before the press gets wind of this."

Simon suddenly grew alert, and stopped watching the play of opposing temperaments and personalities. A sickening thought was tugging at him: Freddie. Freddie had been destroyed by the press, humiliated. He had meant to call him this morning, even though Freddie had claimed he was fine when he spoke to him on Thursday. He would have gotten around to it if Wunnicke hadn't called him in. He'd call later.

"The press," he said scornfully. "Of course! If someone has a grudge against Endicott's, this is a pretty good way to embarrass us."

"Oh, it's worse than that, *Mister* Haden-Jones." Sarah spat. "Didn't you look at *all* of the signs?"

"No, I came straight up."

170

"Well, there was another one that said 'Endicott's Pads Reserves.'"

"What?" Simon was appalled.

"You heard me. Somehow, someone has leaked the information about our new in-house policy, and now it's being paraded around in public on red and blue signs." Her face was distorted with rage.

"My God." Simon had hated that filthy idea of deceiving consigners and buyers from the moment he heard it. Could it be happening that it was bringing down the place he so revered, his citadel, his *life*? His eyes and Sarah's locked in a complicated exchange of accusation, anger, and hatred.

Wunnicke glared in the general direction of the front of the building, and gestured in the air. "Alex is on his way down from Greenwich. I sent my car for him. Now, I want the two of you to handle this with the reporters. Decide on your statement with Alex in advance, and don't mess it up."

Behind the witless command, Simon could feel the man's agitation. He was so used to control, so contemptuous of ambiguity—and here was a situation with all of the form and substance of silly putty. Simon merely sighed and said, "Yes, sir." Sarah marched over to Wunnicke, stood squarely in front of him, and fixed him with a riveting gaze.

"You know you can rely on me. I'll do my best to discredit these...perverts. She turned on her short heels and strode out without a glance at Simon or Harris Tompkins, who sat miserably alone, trying to control a fit of dyspepsia. Simon followed her out of the office and walked quickly behind her, catching up halfway down the long corridor of Picasso prints. Her grabbed her arm, and she wheeled with such force that he was astonished. *"What,"* she asked angrily, *"do...you...want?"* They glared at each other, and Simon found his breath coming in short gasps.

"I want you to behave with a modicum of courtesy, Miss

Dean. We are in this together. We are officers of Endicott's, and we are confronted with the necessity of lying about your morally dubious reserve policy, at the very least. I'll help you now, and I'll be loyal to Endicott's in spite of my personal feelings. I ask that you do the same. This is not the time or the place for us to be divided." She tried to wrest her arm away, but he held fast. He could feel the coiled tension, and it occurred to him that she might strike him. Suddenly, she relaxed, and looked very young and vulnerable, but the look passed in an instant.

"All right. Now let me go, please." She turned, and the confrontation was over as unexpectedly as it had begun.

Simon fell in behind her at a slower pace. My God, he thought. I don't know who young women are any more. Selena, Selena. Do I know you any better than I know this monstrous, dishonest M.B.A. person? Of course I do. There is always the instinctual feeling, and everything I feel or have felt for you is blind, dumb, ancient instinct—with a late twentieth-century intellectual overlay, of course. Suddenly, he turned and headed for his own office. He walked up the steps to the third floor, lost in disturbing thoughts. He punched in the code for the door, and plunged into the long dark corridor towards his sanctum. The corridor was black and smelled of musty heat, but he didn't turn on the lights, thinking that the almost blind walk might help him to compose himself and think through the situation. As he let himself in to his office, the usual warming sense of being home and safe and in control didn't come to him, for the first time he could remember.

"Damn," he uttered as he banged his leg on the red wing chair. "Damn, damn." He knew he had to work with Sarah Dean and Alex Putnam soon, and they all had to appear calm, unruffled, controlled, and most of all, truthful. "Now, just what explanation will cover all of that?" he muttered.

172

He turned on his lamp and sat down at his desk, realizing he would have only a few minutes at best before Alex and Sarah were together. He wanted to go to the press office armed with a strategy, a statement, before confronting the Hydra. He picked up his quill pen, willing wisdom into his fingers, but he made only odd figures on the paper before him. This incident was perplexing because of the messages on the signs, which were obviously inside information. So there was an informant—an antiques "mole" or even two—inside Endicott's. But who? And the thing that didn't fit was the picketers: young Blacks and Hispanics, mostly.

That they had anything to do with Endicott's was not only doubtful, but unbelievable. If the unions had called this demonstration, perhaps. But no union had anything specifically to do with the issues that were being announced oh-so-publicly to passersby—and no doubt, to the New York television viewing and newspaper reading audience later in the day. And the three complaints were so dissimilar! Sexual harassment (he wrote it in calligraphic letters, and drew a horizontal column under it); reserve padding (again, the elegant inscription); and unfair termination policies (he winced at the probably unintentional double entendre and thought of Walter Everest's ugly suicide).

"What is this, a consortium?" he sighed. All three complaints couldn't possibly come from any one person or group or department within Endicott's. He felt instinctively that, to effectively undermine the protesters, he had to understand who was aggrieved and why. Making elegant swirls with his quill didn't help. He couldn't grasp any connection. Then he turned his thoughts to another facet of the problem. Who might benefit from these disclosures? Who could benefit from discrediting Endicott's? Bronte's? Ridiculous. And Sarah Dean couldn't be right about Walter Everest's family; everything had been done to help them financially. If not them, who? Who cares enough to embar-rass....He was interrupted by the ringing phone. Damn.

"Hello. Yes, I'll be right down." Still turning the madden-ing clues over in his mind, he put the paper into his top drawer, left his office, and took the back stairs to the press office.

"Well, Simon. It seems we have a bit of a situ-*a*-tion to deal with...again." Alex had looked up from his conversation with Sarah as he entered the office, and Simon knew instinc-tively that they had been discussing him. Sarah averted her eyes. "I've already called Gretchen Gregg [the antiques col-umnist for *The New York Times* with whom the press office, indeed all the players in the auction world, had a continuing daily dialogue] at home in East Hampton and she laughed! Said to let her know what it was all about when the dust settled." Simon noticed that Alex looked dissipated despite his tan. Alex leaned back in his chair and began snapping his suspenders nervously. "What do you think we should say? Wunnicke wants you out front." He glanced meaning-fully at Sarah.

Simon, whose mind had been going over the messages on the signs once again, cleared his throat. "I think we should completely avoid addressing the complaints, and treat the whole incident lightly." Sarah's head shot up, and she looked at him with an incredulous contempt.

"You mean, let them *get by* with it?"

"Miss Dean. The demonstrators aren't getting by with anything. They are couching some complaints that unfor-tunately are grounded in fact, or could be. And we have absolutely no idea who is behind it. By treating the episode seriously, we will merely add credence to the complaints. I think Alex will agree." Privately, he was thinking of Grace Peabody and his promise of no publicity before the sale of the Cadwalader.

174

"Absolutely. We aren't going to sink to the level of some bastard Chicano kids, for God's sake! That's just elementary psychology." Alex hadn't deduced that the sexual harassment sign was intended for him, seeing it, as Wunnicke had, as a gender complaint. Still....

Two lights on Alex's phone lit up simultaneously. He snapped up the receiver. "Endicott's press...Yes, we know about the picketers. We'll make a formal statement at—let's see (he consulted his watch)—1 p.m. at the main entrance. Yeah...yeah...Have your cameraman on the south side. Yes, we'll have a written statement prepared." He switched to the other line and repeated the message with slight variations. When he hung up, he sighed. "Okay, let's go. I'll draft a short press release incorporating your statement. Of course, none of my interns is available to help me today—all at the beach, I suppose." He gave Sarah a sardonic smile. "If you can give me a rough idea of what you'd like to say, I'll write it out and get Wunnicke's okay." Sarah shifted in her chair.

"*I'll* get Mr. Wunnicke's okay," she stated flatly.

Simon said, "I'd like to say something to the effect that we're happy to have such worthy entertainment provided for us on an otherwise tedious Saturday in August."

"Okay, good." Alex scribbled. "What else?"

"And that...Mr. Wunnicke has often expressed his ardent desire to learn break dancing."

Alex stopped writing abruptly, looked at Simon, and started roaring with laughter. Even Sarah couldn't suppress a smile.

"*Great!* That's great—*if* he'll let you say that." Sarah, who knew Wunnicke's particular acrobatic limitations, couldn't help seeing a picture of E. Martin in a suit and vest whirling on the sidewalk, his white, naked legs scissoring clumsily.

"Okay, folks. We've got 45 minutes. Oh, Simon—have you got a tie and jacket? Image, you know."

What a profession is public relations, Simon thought. It must change the brain chemistry somehow.

"A jacket? Yes, I have an extra in my office. But I don't have a dress shirt or tie."

"Never mind. Here's my all-purpose Arnold Sulka silk." Alex rose and went to a hook on the back of his office door, removing a tie from it. "The polo shirt won't show with this on."

Simon nodded and rose to leave. "Do you need me for anything else?"

"Not until 1:00. Sarah, is this statement okay with you?" Sarah nodded unhappily. "And Simon, please stay available. Just in case."

"Of course I will." Simon shot out of the office, clasping the borrowed silk tie.

XOXOX

After the press conference, which Simon thought had been a silly circus—the demonstrators had so little to say, the reporters were so appreciative of his humor—he returned to his office feeling oddly let down. The exhilaration of the morning had vanished, not to be recovered, and no sense of victory held him. It had been so easy: the powerful against the powerless, the well spoken against the barely articulate, the well dressed against the ill clad. He'd made fools of the young people, and their cause or causes had been secondary, trammeled, forgotten. Yet...they had been right. Their placards spoke the truth. Then what was he then—a well-dressed puppet? Of Wunnicke?

"Nuts," he said aloud. "Nuts. Nuts." I had to do this, he thought, that's all. After the local news airs tonight, and tomorrow's papers are read and thrown out, the affair will be forgotten—I devoutly hope.

He removed Alex's tie and hung it with his jacket in the closet. He couldn't wait to get out into the fresh air. He had seen enough of Alex and Sarah and Wunnicke for one day. He left his office, strode down the corridor, and took the steps at as rapid a pace as he could. He'd shake off this feeling. He'd be fine before tonight. *Les Liaisons Dangereuses* suddenly seemed an apt choice of play.

When he reached the double doors, he found that Al, the security guard, had locked them, turned off the lights, and left. Simon fumbled for his key, leaning against the glass to use the waning sunlight. As he did so, something caught his eye. Down the street, the last stragglers from the demonstration were loading their signs into a battered van with a logo on the side depicting a man's face and a giant pizza. He could just make out "...cky's pizza." The driver, an Hispanic youth, was hurrying them along. Suddenly, he smiled and waved to someone on the other side of the street, someone Simon couldn't quite see. For reasons he would consider to the end of his life, he watched, transfixed, pressing his cheek against the glass, until the hurrying figure on his side of the street became visible.

She didn't turn, but he didn't have to see her face. He knew it was Selena.

)O(O(

The late afternoon sun sent shafts of light onto his face, and dappled the trees and building fronts with yellow. But Simon didn't notice. He stumbled along, sweating profusely, his throat constricted, his heart thudding monotonously, noisily against his chest wall. He felt a pain that he could not localize, an anger so great that if he acknowledged it, let it out, it would immolate him. He'd never been violent, but the thought of destroying something came again and again.

How can I accept betrayal? he thought. He felt so many emotions, all overlapping, and had no way to sort them out.

It was as if a rusty Pandora's box had opened, and all the evil demons had come rushing out, bringing everything ugly and vile with them. He kicked furiously at a plastic cup scuddering across the street, and when a taxi nearly hit him at an intersection, he banged his fist angrily on the hood so hard it hurt.

"Hey, *asshole!*" The cabbie had extended his third finger obscenely before taking off, tires screeching.

Simon stormed around several blocks before he came to his senses enough to look at a street sign. He'd gone six blocks beyond his building.

Got to go home—take an aspirin or have a drink or something, he thought. He found his building, and butted past the doorman, who said, "Mr. Haden-Jones, there's...." But Simon waved him off. He entered the elevator, and began breathing deeply to regain control of himself.

When the door opened on his floor, the first thing he saw was a pair of uniformed policemen leaning against the wall. Oh, God, he thought. Not the damn demonstration.

"Simon Haden-Jones?"

"Yes," Simon answered disgustedly, going to his door and inserting the key. "The demonstration at Endicott's is over, officers, and I am...."

"Sir, we're here...well...do you know a Frederick Trosper?"

"Trosper? Trosper? No, I...." Suddenly there was a faint glimmer in his mind.

"He also had with him some mail addressed to Freddie...let's see...Trowbridge."

"Of course I know him! And what do you mean, *had?*" Suddenly, Simon felt crazy, out of his mind.

The other officer spoke, "I'm afraid there's been an accident."

178

He remembered Freddie's beating. "What kind of an accident?" he asked dully.

"Well, sir, Mr. Trosper...."

"Stop calling him that ridiculous name!" Simon snapped.

"Mr. Trowbridge, then...well...I'm afraid he's dead."

Falling bricks and shapes, buildings disintegrating, planets imploding, colors screaming into spirals in his head, black slashes everywhere. "Dead? What do you mean...dead?"

"Looks like a possible suicide, sir. We've been waiting for you because we need someone to identify the body."

Simon nodded dumbly, took one step, then fell to his knees in front of the disconcerted policemen.

)O(O(

"Are you sure you're up to this now, Mr. *Hay*-dun-Jones? We could come back tomorrow." The policeman's ruddy face peered over the car seat at Simon as the police car moved downtown on Lexington Avenue.

Tomorrow. Would there be any tomorrow? "No, I'm fine now. Thank you." He felt anything but fine, but he didn't think that the relentless progression of days known as "tomorrow" would effect any change in his state of mind. Ever.

"Okay, then. Whaddever you say." The officer faced forward, exchanging a significant glance with the driver, and Simon leaned back against the seat, closing his eyes and pressing his fingers against his temples. A sea of images danced behind his closed eyes: Freddie, in his silly bowler hat, his head thrown back, laughing with Judy Dunleigh at a reception; Freddie, the flamboyant art history student with the brilliant wit and encyclopedic knowledge; Freddie, with his face purple and distended, in a hospital bed.

Oh, God, Freddie. Why did you do it?

He was trying to numb himself, but a couplet he'd

179

learned at Hotchkiss kept running through his mind:

The grave's a fine and private place,
But none I think do there embrace.

The grave. But he, Simon Haden-Jones, was in the full of his life! And so was Freddie. Death was not welcome here! How could Freddie have danced with Death, locked himself in the eternal embrace? How could he have chosen Death?

"We're here."

Simon flicked open his eyes and a ribbon of pain moved like lightning across his forehead. He looked up at the ugly stone facade of the city morgue. One policeman got out and opened the door for him, and the two walked up the steps with him between them, making him feel rather like a prisoner. One held the door open for him, then indicated a scarred oak bench in the hall. "Wait there, please, sir."

He sank down heavily, and the policemen walked down the hall, their heels clattering, stopped before a glass-paneled door, and rapped. He could seem them talking to a seated man in a suit who glanced his way and nodded. Presently, the man came out and walked toward him.

"Mr. Haden-Jones? I'm Detective Mallozzi. Sorry you had to come down."

"That's all right. I want to help. It's not your fault. Are you sure? Are you sure it's Freddie Trowbridge?"

"That's why we have to ask you. We're never sure until a relative or friend tells us. But we couldn't find any relatives. Shall we go?"

"Where is he?"

"Downstairs in storage."

Storage.

"Follow me, please." Detective Mallozzi walked a step ahead of him and indicated an elevator. As they entered, Simon saw an empty gurney, and his stomach wrenched. The elevator, lit by a single fluorescent tube, was dingy and smelled of formaldehyde. Mallozzi watched him carefully as they descended.

When the door opened, the detective said, "To the right." The corridor was spotlessly clean, but to Simon, used to deep Aubusson carpets and damask draperies, it was hideous, like a passage in Hell. The smell assaulted him continually. Almost like a hospital, and yet....

Mallozzi paused before two swinging stainless steel doors. "Are you ready?" Simon nodded. The detective opened the doors, and Simon saw a wall of large drawers. Mallozzi walked to one and opened it gently.

Simon's first impression was of a bluish foot with a gift tag on it, and he almost burst out in hysterical laughter. As he moved closer, he could see the torso and the right side of the colorless face.

Simon gasped and tears stung his eyes. He dug his nails into his palms so hard that they nearly bled.

"Yes."

"Are you sure?"

"Yes."

Mallozzi closed the drawer gently, and patted Simon's shoulder. "Let's go."

The ascent was passed in silence. Back in his office, Mallozzi sat Simon down, walked around his desk and pulled a flask of bourbon from a bottom drawer.

"Here. Have a drink. It'll help."

Simon looked at him intently, then drank straight from the flask. The searing shock of the alcohol helped him to cast out the hideous scene below.

"It's rough, I know it is."

"What happened to him?"

"He jumped—or maybe fell—from his apartment roof late last night. I guess we'll never know for sure." Mallozzi took the bottle back, and poured some bourbon into a water glass. "Do you know if he has any relatives around?"

"No, I don't think so. He never mentioned anyone."

"Do you know why he might have wanted to take his own life?"

Simon nodded. "He's just been pilloried—humiliated—in the press for an involvement with a...." Simon choked on the words. It would come out anyway. He might as well tell the story.

"Yes?"

"With a pimp in some set-up with boy dancers—prostitutes, actually."

"Was your friend a homosexual?"

Simon paled. "I believe so. But he was very discreet."

"In the newspaper is discreet?" The detective arched his eyebrows.

"I mean...until now."

The two fell quiet. Then Mallozzi spoke. "Smoke?"

"No, I don't."

"More bourbon?"

"No, I'm all right. Really."

"Okay." Mallozzi pushed back his chair and opened the middle drawer of his desk.

"He left a letter—for you. It's how we found you. But we couldn't reach you by phone, so the officers went to wait. Are they glad you weren't out of town!" Mallozzi hazarded a crooked grin as he handed the torn envelope to Simon.

"It's been opened!" Simon said with dismay.

"Dead people have no right to privacy."

Simon looked at the envelope for a long time, and at the jagged tear across the top. Couldn't they have opened it properly? he thought angrily. Then he removed the sheet of paper and slowly unfolded it on the desk. The writing was spidery and wandering.

Simon, mon cher ami,

The thunder in the glen is deafening, and I must depart. Keep my treasures, and love your girl. Be wonderful for both of us.

Á bientót,
Freddie

Simon could hear Freddie's voice. He looked hard at Mallozzi to keep from weeping.

"Well, I think that's all for now, Mr. Haden-Jones. I'm sorry about your friend. Thanks again for coming. The officers will drive you home."

Simon said heavily, "No, I'll get a taxi. Can I keep the note?"

"Not yet. It'll have to be available for the police report. You can pick up all of his things after the autopsy."

The room reeled. Autopsy. Did death go on every day while he was at Endicott's, or at home, or driving his Mercedes? Was this the same world?

"I'll take care of him," he said stiffly.

Mallozzi handed him a card. "Here's my number. Call me tomorrow." He again patted Simon's shoulder. "I'll walk you out."

As they went along the hall, Simon realized that the detective was about his age, and even his height. How different their lives were. At the door, Simon shook Mallozzi's hand, thanked him, and asked, "Tell me: How did you get into this line of work?" The detective stubbed out his cigarette, shrugged, and said, "Everybody winds up somewhere."

Chapter 20

Selena coiled and uncoiled her long hair, pinning it this way and that on top of her head. Simon likes it up, as Neal had, she thought ruefully. But she didn't know what she would say to Simon other than the pleasantries. She felt both guilty and exhilarated, and the combination created a sort of overstrung tiredness. She was glad he had chosen to take her to the theatre for their date. They didn't have to say much during the course of a play, and she could plead fatigue when it was over. Oh, it was all too difficult! The picketing had been upsetting to her sensibilities, even though Anna had been elated because several television crews had come. It had been such an uncivilized idea.

How she would love to be home in Florence in her room, with the bells from the convent on the hill tolling, looking up from her bed at the painted ceiling. She could remember every figure in the lovely scene depicted there: cherubs, clouds, mythological figures. It seemed so far away! She glanced up and saw only the long crack on the painted white plaster of her apartment ceiling.

She glanced at her watch: 6:30. She had half an hour before Simon arrived. Suddenly, homesickness welled up in her, as potent as nausea. It would be after midnight in Florence, but it was Saturday. She had to go home, to touch home! She picked up the phone and pushed the sequence of buttons.

"*Buon giorno! Villa Fraccese.*"

"*Buon giorno! Signore Fraccese, favore?*"

"*Si, momento.*" She didn't bother to identify herself, for

she never knew which maid might answer, or which might be a recent addition to the staff of the wonderful house. After a short pause, her father's laughing voice come over the wire. "*Si?*" Selena heard voices and music in the background.

"Papa? It's Selena." She heard him muffle the phone with his hand and quiet someone.

"*Chi è?*"

"Selena, Papa."

"Oh, how wonderful! We are just speaking of you and your big *avventura* in New York."

"Who's with you, Papa?."

"We are having a big party for the local vineyard owner, Sr. Novatello, and his wife." There was a burst of laughter, and Selena heard a concertina playing. "He's playing his... how is it said, 'squeeze-box'?"

"I wish I were there with you, Papa! Is Mama there?"

"Yes, and she looks beautiful." She heard an exaggerated kiss being blown. Oh, it was too much! She in this squalid apartment and misery and heat while a wonderful party was going on at her home. She felt like crying.

"Are you coming home soon, *cara?*" Her father's voice had the dreamy quality of one whose wine consumption had exceeded his limits.

"I don't think I'll have time before school."

"Oh, what a pity. We miss you (*Si, si, momento, Cosima.)*" She felt his attention turning away from her, back to his guests. How alone and miserable she was! "Papa, we had the demonstration at Endicott's today."

"What? Oh, good for you, I hope it does good." His voice was distracted, and Selena thought petulantly that he hadn't even heard her, and maybe didn't care.

"*Cara*, join us from New York. You have a bottle of good red wine, *si?*"

186

"Yes, of course."

"*Bene*. Go get it, open it, and we'll toast together right now. You'll almost be here with us." She could hear the laughter and people clapping.

"Yes, I'll get it." She rose hastily, went to the kitchen, took a bottle of Antinori Tignanello from the cupboard, and opened it quickly. She poured it into her one crystal wine glass, and hurried back to the phone. But the connection had been broken. She replaced the receiver, sat down solemnly, and raised her glass, toasting all that was beautiful and happy in her home.

When seven o'clock had come and gone, she grew restless. Simon wasn't the sort to be late, and she certainly didn't expect it of him. She'd had several glasses of the fine red wine by then, and rather than feeling relaxed, she felt dizzy and cranky. She flipped on the television and sat on the futon where, after a few minutes of aimless channel changing and gloomy thoughts about the dilemma she'd gotten herself into, she drifted off, her head lolling back against the wall.

She awakened completely disoriented and groggy. "What time is...?" The ghostly flickers from the television were the only light in the room. She reached clumsily for the lamp, finally managing to turn it on. Her watch read 11:10. She shook her head and looked at it again. 11:10. What had happened? Had he come and she been asleep? Was the phone off the hook? She checked it quickly for a dial tone, which she heard immediately. She stood up and rubbed her eyes. What could have happened? She went to the window and looked down at the street, half expecting to see the old Mercedes with him leaning against it, arms akimbo, looking up. But there was nothing. Suddenly, movement on the television screen caught her eye. It was the afternoon scene in front of Endicott's, and she could recognize Lorenzo and

Donna. She dived for the sound switch.

A young reporter, obviously a summer understudy, was pushing a microphone awkwardly toward a serious and self-possessed Simon. "...a spokesman for Endicott's, Simon Haden-Jones: What do you say to the charges brought by these young demonstrators here today?"

"Groundless. Of course they have no basis in fact whatso-ever, but we do thank these young people for entertaining us on such a normally dull Saturday afternoon." The reporter smiled appreciatively as Simon shifted his position and ran his hand through his hair. Selena was astonished at how handsome he looked on camera, how tall and patrician. He could have been an actor, she thought fleetingly.

The reporter persisted: "Then you deny these allegations?"

"Absolutely." (Selena's teeth clenched. How could he? He knew!)

"Have you any idea why Endicott's was targeted for a public demonstration?"

Simon was quiet for a moment, then said, "We have had a very tragic death of our long-time president, a type of situation that often gives rise to rumor. And any industry that is producing enormous profits is bound to come under some sort of unwanted scrutiny."

"Then you think that someone with an axe to grind may be behind this?"

"I wouldn't care to speculate." With this, Simon gave a dismissive nod, indicating that the interview was at an end.

"Thank you, Mr. Haden-Jones. This is Allison Palmer reporting from Endicott's Art Auction House in Manhattan. Back to you, Jerry." Selena noted several of the demonstra-tors mugging in the background.

She rubbed her eyes, unable to distinguish between waking and sleeping states, between the televised Endicott's and the very real scene she had witnessed, between the

188

Simon she knew and the one who had told patent lies on the late night news, between the Selena who came to intern at Endicott's and the unhappy moralist she was now. Had she gone through a looking glass or down a rabbit hole? Was she dreaming all of it?

She turned off the set, and tried to bring order to her confused feelings. But the events of the day were still distorted, dreamlike, phantasmagorical. Had Simon come for her? Where was he? How could he have lied? How could he not have come? She'd just seen him! Her head was thick and her throat dry. There was nothing she could do. It was too late to call anyone, let alone him, whom she wouldn't have felt comfortable ringing up on the most normal of days. Her eyes began to sting, and she realized she was crying. Profoundly unhappy, she made her way to the bedroom, where she removed her clothes, shook out her hair, and climbed into bed, shivering in the heat of the New York August. What shall I do? she thought over and over, staring at the blackness above her. Oh, dear Papa, what have I done?

)(О)(О)(

The telephone seemed to be shrieking when it awakened her the next morning. Head pounding, she stumbled to the living room.

"*Well?* Did you pull it off? Did you have fun?"

"Oh, Anna. Oh, God, Anna, no. He...wait, let me sit down." She deposited herself heavily on the futon. "He didn't come."

"What do you *mean?* Did you fold, and break the date?"

"No, Anna. He just didn't come."

"I don't believe it, Seels! Did he say why? Was it the demonstration?"

"No. Oh, Anna. He didn't even call."

189

"*Wait* a minute. He didn't come *or* call? Oh, no, it can't be. Simon Haden-Jones would never do that."

"Well, I fell asleep and didn't wake up until the eleven o'clock news was on, and he hadn't come or called."

Anna exhaled sharply and said, "Then something must be terribly wrong. He must've *died* or something."

"Don't say that!"

"Did you call him?"

"No—it was too late. I just couldn't."

"But it's ridiculous. Look—I'll get the *Times* and bring some bagels. Be over in fifteen minutes."

"I'm not...very well."

"*So?* I'm coming. Bye." Anna rang off hastily, leaving Selena with a protest dying on her lips.

She hung up, shook out her hair, went back to the bedroom, and slipped into some shorts, sandals, and a silk tee. It was hard to remember the previous day in any proper emotional sequence. The demonstration, which she'd had to see despite her intention of staying away; the dismay and upset she felt at the way the demonstrators had actually appeared, more like crackpots or publicity seekers than serious spokesmen; then speaking with her father—had she?—and feeling so isolated and shut out. Then the delicate effort of preparing an emotional mask for a theater date with Simon that had....

Suddenly, she realized how frightening it really was that Simon hadn't come. She couldn't say with any certainty that she hadn't slept through a ringing phone. She shook her head with the effort of understanding the puzzle. Going to the kitchen, she measured coffee into the pot and realized how much her head ached. As the coffeemaker sputtered into life, she walked to the window and gazed out moodily. New York City on a humid August Sunday morning did nothing to raise her spirits, or to cure her heart's unease.

Had she really looked at this vista and felt something wonderful was about to happen? When was that—in June?

Her reverie was interrupted by the insistent ringing of the downstairs bell announcing Anna's arrival. She buzzed her friend in and heard the whir of the elevator's motor. Soon Anna appeared at the door, red-faced and laden with a newspaper and a beige bag.

"*God!*" Anna yelled as she dropped everything just inside the door. "It's hotter than yesterday." The girls embraced briefly. Anna picked up the bag and made her way to the kitchen, while Selena retrieved the *Times*. "Coffee! Quick!" Anna took out the mugs and snapped her fingers impatiently as the last of the water dripped through the filter. She called to Selena, "Look at the metropolitan section and see if we got covered." From the refrigerator she took out the cream cheese and began to slather it on the bagels, making a little tray of breakfast, which she carried into the living room. Selena was scanning the pages of the *Times*.

Anna sat next to her on the futon. "He's not home," she announced.

"Who?"

"Simon Haden-Jones."

Selena jumped up, nearly upsetting Anna's tray. "How do you know?"

"I called him." She took a bite of pumpernickel bagel.

"You *what?*"

"He doesn't have an answering machine, either. Or at least it wasn't turned on."

"Anna, how could you?"

"Hey—I want to know where he is. Don't you?"

"But what if he'd been there? What would you have said?"

"I'd have said, 'Sorry, wrong number.'"

"Oh." Selena suddenly felt disoriented again. "Anna, what do you think happened?"

191

"Seely, I just can't imagine—*oh, my God!* Here it is! Look! It's a whole column." She began to read aloud: "'Endicott's Demonstrators Allege Illegal Practices.' Oh, *wow, wow, wow!* Hooray for the first amendment!" She got up and began to dance around while Selena read the rest of the story.

"Anna, it says in the last paragraph that the *Times* will begin a three-part series on pricing practices in the art auction market on August 27."

"No!" Anna stopped dancing and put both fists to her mouth. Tears sprang to her eyes. "Selena, we did it. I just can't believe it. They'll find out everything. About the reserves and Walter Everest. Everything." She fell silent.

Selena asked gently, "Will they?"

"Yes—except maybe about Alex Putnam and his desk jobs—but *who cares?* I've got to call Julio and Loretta." She lunged for the phone, and an excited conversation ensued. When she hung up, she took up her mug of coffee and looked at Selena intently. "This could be the most wonderful thing I'll ever do in my life. Like Daniel Ellsberg and the Pentagon papers. My father talked about that all the time."

"Who?" Selena asked innocently.

"He...oh, well, never mind."

"I'm glad. You're so smart, Anna."

Anna shrugged. "Lucky, you mean. The demonstration wasn't that great." She let out a great whoop of exultation. "Now there's only one thing left to do."

"What?" Selena asked.

"Find Simon Haden-Jones."

XOXOX

Monday at Endicott's was unusual. Simon did not appear. People speaking in groups in the corridors jumped apart guiltily when anyone approached. Red lights indicated inter

192

office phones heavily in use. There was unusual scurrying in and out of the executive suite. And the air conditioning malfunctioned, and the humid stickiness intensified the atmosphere of anxious conspiracy.

Gloom hung heavily about Selena. She sat numbly at her desk, proofreading the catalogue copy for the "Important American Furniture and Decorative Items" sale, which would feature the Cadwalader chair. The photograph was superb. Richly and newly upholstered in blue damask for the sale, the chair radiated grandeur even from its likeness. Selena bit her lip as she looked at the hairy paws and remembered the dark evening when Simon held her hand over them and kissed her. Where was he? What was wrong? She blinked back tears and read the chair's description.

> The General John Cadwalader extremely rare and important Chippendale carved mahogany wing armchair, made by Thomas Affleck, the carving by James Reynolds, Philadelphia, 1770. Exuberant carving on the skirt, where acanthus leaves embellish its serpentine form. Estimate $700,000/$900,000.

Someone new would own the Cadwalader chair soon, and it probably would go to a wealthy patron's home. But what would they know of it, other than its cost and beauty? Could they ever know what Simon knew when he reached back across the centuries to touch the very hand of its creator?

She stopped reading, rose, and went once again to stand in the doorway of Simon's dark and musty office. There was still no sign of him. Heart heavy, she walked into the warren that housed Arabella. The older girl looked stricken.

"Arabella, have you had any word from Mr. Haden-Jones?"

Arabella shook her head and her red curls slapped her cheeks softly. Suddenly, she began to cry.

Selena, so reserved, was taken aback "What *is* it, Arabella? Has something happened to him?"

"No, no. But his friend...that fancy man from Bronte's..." Another great sob. "He died on Friday night."

"Oh?"

"He, he, he...jumped off his roof." By now Arabella's eyes were as pink as a rabbit's.

"You mean the one who got into that dreadful scandal with the prostitution ring?" Arabella nodded, dabbing ineffectually at her eyes with a shredding tissue. "Were they close? I didn't know."

"I think they were best friends."

Selena thought for a moment. This could account for the broken date and Simon's unexplained absence. But it nevertheless was so unlike him. Everything in his breeding would tell him to call, to keep her from worrying. She pushed away the notion that he might have had some sort of breakdown.

Arabella continued to sputter helplessly. "And now this mess with the *Times* and the investigation. Oh, it'll *kill* him, Selena. And he's so *good*."

By now, she was lost to tears, and all Selena could do was pat her shoulder and mumble, "I'm sorry. I'm sorry." Rigid with guilt, she marched stiffly back to her desk, staring straight ahead. I don't know what I feel. Why can't I tell right from wrong anymore? Suddenly, the phone rang and shattered her anxious thoughts.

"Seels." A conspiratorial whisper. "Did you know Simon's friend killed himself Friday night?"

"Yes, I just heard."

"We were so darn busy reading about our demonstration that I didn't bother to look at the previous page. The press office is a *mess*. Two auction house scandals in one paper— it's fascinating. Oh—and nobody here has a *clue* about the demonstration. They're all barking up very wrong trees."

194

Then, apparently because someone had walked into her office, she suddenly said, "Okay, bye," and ended the call.

Selena returned the phone to the cradle and sighed. She felt somewhat responsible for Simon's plight, and it loomed at that moment far more important to her than righting of the wrongs of Endicott's. Suddenly, she had an uncontrollable desire to see the story of Simon's friend's death. The press office seemed the worst place to look for it today. She returned to Arabella's desk and asked for the Sunday *Times*.

"I didn't bring it in," Arabella sniffled. Afraid that a new wave of crying would overcome the girl, Selena left rapidly. She walked down the long corridor, peering surreptitiously at desks. At last she saw a fat pile of newspapers on the desk of Mike O'Donnell in appraisals. She went in boldly and grabbed the front section for Sunday, darting like a hungry sea bird after its prey. She was about to dash away when her scruples overcame her. She went back and wrote a quick note: "Borrowed the *Times*. Will return." Feeling like a thief, she ran down the corridor and went to her desk to read.

The small headline on the front page read: "Bronte's Expert Dies in Fall. See p. 6." She turned to the story, disarranging the pages in her haste. There was a photo, and the face that smiled out from under a dapper Homburg looked impish and intelligent. She read the copy hungrily:

> Frederick Trowbridge, 41, a colorful figure for two decades in the New York auction world and head of the French furniture department at Bronte's, was found dead early yesterday morning behind his apartment building on Bank Street. According to police, he jumped or fell from the roof to his death.

A friend said that Trowbridge was depressed over a scandal in which he had been implicated.

Mr. Trowbridge created the French furniture department at Bronte's, and was responsible for bringing to the U.S. several major collections owned by French noble families. Known for his wit, he gained access to legendary French chateaux and palaces and persuaded owners to consign their possessions for auction outside the country.

He was born Frederick Trosper in Ottawa, Ill., where he attended public schools. There are no immediate survivors. Services and burial were private.

Selena put the paper down quietly. No immediate survivors. This probably meant that Simon—she wanted to cry—was taking care of his friend's funeral arrangements. Alone. She felt shame and complete disdain for herself, and for her and Anna's childish enterprise. She would have liked to hold Simon and tell him, "Sorry, sorry, my dear man, I'm so sorry," over and over again. If only he would come back!

But he didn't. Nor did he call Arabella or the press office. By close of day on Tuesday, every one at Endicott's was discussing the strange and atypical disappearance of Simon Haden-Jones. And on the eve of the auction of the most important piece he'd ever acquired! Selena felt sick and miserable. Again, the thought that he might have suffered a breakdown came to her.

Then, suddenly on Wednesday morning, there he was.

Chapter 21

Selena dragged listlessly into the office Wednesday morning. As she trudged down the hallway, Arabella suddenly appeared in front of her. "He's *here*," she whispered. Selena nodded a "thank you," and quickened her step toward the doorway of Simon's office, where light shone forth for the first time in days. But she stopped short in the corridor, overwhelmed by doubt. As much as she wanted to see him—if only to assure herself that he was all right—she didn't have an idea of what say. Yet her desire for confirmation of his return was stronger than her confusion, and so she stepped slowly through the door frame.

He looked gaunt and pale, sitting there with his quill pen scratching across papers spread on his desk. Dark hollows had appeared under his eyes. She cleared her throat timidly, and his eyes moved up to meet hers.

"Simon...I...I'm very glad you're back." He nodded, not taking his eyes from her face.

"Please come in." He didn't smile. His aspect was one of a man who'd been imprisoned without light, food, or water for a long time, and was testing himself, his faculties, and his spirit to see if by any miracle they were as before. "Please sit for a moment."

She perched tentatively on the arm of the velvet wing chair. He continued to look at her with such a dreadful sadness in his eyes that she wanted to cry or run out. Eventually, he put down the ink-stained feather, leaned back, and spoke. "I'm sorry about the theater on Saturday. I was called away. I tried to phone before I left, but your line was busy."

She remembered the call to Villa Fraccese. "Later, I...I just couldn't."

"It's all right." Once again, she was touched by his intense, brooding look.

"I...I've been through quite a lot," he admitted. "I'm not quite myself."

"I understand. About your friend."

He interrupted her with a quick wave, as if the allusion was too painful to bear. Again, he fixed her with his intense stare. Then he rose, walked past her and closed the door. She tensed in the charged atmosphere.

When he spoke, his voice was so low she wasn't sure she had heard him. "How could you, Selena?" She turned quickly, and looked up into his sad eyes. "How could you betray me?"

She flinched. "I don't understand."

"Oh, Selena. I saw you. With the demonstrators last Saturday." She was overcome with such shame and humiliation that she could only nod dumbly. Simon took a breath as if the act hurt every bone in his tall body. He went on: "Don't you know what harm you've caused? Working at Endicott's is a great privilege, a trust—and you've betrayed it."

The fluttering of her heart in her chest was like a cornered bird, desperate to flee from its cage as a predator advanced. She mumbled an incoherent "Sorry...."

Suddenly, he was in front of her, pulling her to her feet. His probing eyes engaged hers and she saw the same fever in them she'd seen the night he had spoken so passionately about the chair.

"Don't you understand?" His grip on her shoulders tightened. "I love you. I want to be with you...." Suddenly he began to kiss her so hard she couldn't breathe. His hands moved down her back and crushed her chest against him. She stood for a moment with her arms hanging limp, too shocked to respond. Then his hands went to her waist and slid up to her breasts. She realized that he was moaning, and she began to fight him. "No, Simon...." She twisted her head and began to beat at him. "*No!*" By now she was mad with terror. She struggled with him, breaking free of his embrace, and ran wildly out of his office, tearing blindly down the corridor with tears streaming from her eyes, past the icy receptionist, down the staircase, sobbing "No, no," to the startled employees and patrons who saw her run through the brass double doors of Endicott's for the very last time.

That night, a Ms. Selena Fraccese boarded an Olympic Airlines jet bound for Athens, the last standby to be ticketed. In her apartment she had left a note for the landlord with instructions to send her deposit to Villa Fraccese, Florence, Italy. She had left the keys with the superintendent, informing him that before the month's end Julio would pick up the futon, the bed, and what he wanted of the makeshift furniture. Her last act before boarding the flight was to mail two letters, one addressed to Anna, and the other to Simon.

XOXOX

My *God* what a summer, Alex Putnam thought as he sank down behind his desk. It was 7:15 p.m. in Endicott's press office, and the phones were only beginning to cease ringing. What do they *expect* of me at this place? The old-boy Greenwich charm can only be sustained for so long. He rose, closed his door, and took out the small silver container of white powder, fingering it idly.

This investigation is going to be a stinker, he thought. They'll probably find out everything about the illegal reserve policy, and who knows what else. Ah, well. He tapped the powder into a line on his desk, scraped it into position with a gold credit card, carefully rolled up the crisp $20 bill, and inhaled deeply, first the right nostril, then the left. A feeling of peace spread through him, and he felt so euphoric and powerful that the investigation was temporarily forgotten.

Alex, old boy—do you really want to be caught with your pants down and your mouth open? He chortled, and dialed his Yale friend Phelpsy Chalmers, a marketing man at one of the leading high-tech firms who, of course, was not there.

Tomorrow, he promised himself. Use the Endicott's name for leverage while it still means something. He closed his eyes and saw downy limbs and the impossible thick hair of a certain young assistant in the pre-Columbian pottery department. I'd like to catch *him* with his pants down and his mouth open, he thought with lascivious pleasure. Erotic thoughts and visions occupied him briefly. Then he picked up the phone. "Hey—still here? Well, listen. Meet me in my office in half an hour. *Tremendous* surprise for you, chickadee. Then we'll have dinner—on me, of course—and hit Club Adonis, okay? Great."

He chuckled as he put down the phone. Now, whom could he get to help him? Bert. Of course. The old night watchman. For $20, he would move the earth and keep quiet. With a phone call, he made hasty arrangements for Bert to meet him in the stacks and bring the key to the locked vault. Alex grinned to himself at his own daring, snapped his suspenders nervously as he walked down the back corridor, rode the lift up, and saw an anxious Bert, key ring dangling from his belt, awaiting him.

"Are you sure this'll be all right, Mr. Putnam?"

"Sure, Bert, sure," he answered expansively. "Just move it back before morning and make sure it's locked up tight, okay?" Bert Looked doubtful.

"Okay, Mr. Putnam. But it's that Catwallatter chair, isn't it? It's awful valuable."

"Now, Bert, would I hurt a mere thread of its damask? I need it for a press release." Alex indicated the lock with some impatience.

Between the two of them, they managed to move the Cadwalader, draped in a sheet, down the lift, through the dark corridor, and into Alex's office. "Thanks, Bert. I'll be through with it in a couple of hours. You can come back for it then." He thrust the twenty at the older man, who nodded worriedly and left.

Alex removed the sheet slowly and looked at the chair. The frame was massive, and it overwhelmed the windowless office, but the bigger the better, he thought. The rich blue Scalamandre silk damask brought out the patina of its gorgeously carved legs.

"Well," Alex said as he sat back, for the moment owner of the most valuable chair in America. "Well, well." A short knock on the door indicated the arrival of Chaz, Alex's current playmate.

"Oh, gawd, it's *wonderful.* Alex, you pervert. How'd you get it down here?" Chaz stepped back and eyed the chair appreciatively.

"Piece of cake. Here, have some heaven." He poured out a line from the silver tin, arranging it as before, but this time it was Chaz who inhaled it. He then sat gingerly on the Cadwalader, and started to laugh. Soon Alex joined in. Then he moved toward Chaz, pushing him back in the seat, and unfastening his trousers. With a singleness of mind seldom seen in his daily work, Alex removed Chaz's trousers and briefs, then stood back to admire the picture. The man in the chair posed and vamped, moving his legs this way and that, under Alex's approving eye. Then Alex dropped to his knees in front of Chaz and said, "Let's show this old chair something it's never seen before." He put his hands on the other man's knees, spreading them, and moved his tongue up the downy thighs to the pulsing muscle at the vertex, loving the look of the tanned flesh against the exquisite blue damask.

XOXOX

Simon hadn't expected her to return that day, but when Thursday came and went with no sign of or word from her, he became concerned. At 4:30, he asked Arabella to call her. "No answer," she reported. His depression deepened as he realized that his loss of control must have frightened her badly. He would speak to her when she came back, and calmly apologize. Perhaps he could make it right. Perhaps.

On Friday morning, he received a telephone call from Anna in the press office. "Mr. Haden-Jones? I've had a note from Selena saying that she has been called home, and asking that I inform you."

Simon answered dully, "Home?"

"Yes, to Florence. She asks that you send any personal possessions she may have left to her at Villa Fraccese, Florence."

There was a long pause. "Mr. Haden-Jones?"

"I see," he answered. "Then she's not coming back?"

"I'm afraid not, sir."

"And she said nothing more specific?"

"No, I'm afraid not."

"Well, thank you, Miss...er...."

"Anna."

"Anna." He replaced the phone and put his hands to his temples.

Anna sighed with relief. The little white lie had required considerable effort, for Selena's note had explained what

202

had happened in some detail, and how upset and confused she was. Another sigh, because she felt nearly as responsible as Simon for Selena's flight.

When the afternoon mail was delivered, Simon noticed the small envelope with Selena's unmistakable script. He turned it over and over, then rose and closed his office door. He opened it slowly, very slowly. It read:

Dear Simon:

I am so sorry to have been the cause of any trouble for you, and I hope you will forgive my leaving my internship two weeks early. You were very kind to me, and I know that the sale of the Cadwalader chair will bring you satisfaction.

Please understand that I only tried to do what I thought was right.

Sincerely,
Selena Fraccese

For the first time since Freddie's death a week earlier, Simon broke down and wept.

XOXOX

"You don't know what I've *been* through to get the date of the cotillion changed!" Mona Elliott lounged in a red caftan on a deck overlooking the sea. She leaned her head back and propped the phone against her ear. "Judy Dunleigh fought me tooth and *nail,* darling, tooth-and-*nail!* Ummmm. Ummmmm. Just a minute, the dogs...(she hastily covered the mouthpiece of the phone and shouted, "Charlemagne! Stop that! Madame de Stael! I...am...*shocked* at you! You *know* drinking from the pool gives you gas!)...What was I saying, darling? Yes, but you know Endicott's *never* has sales before Labor Day. Oh, tosh, darling! Who *says* that the

Labor Day Cotillion has to be on Labor Day? Small minds—
no imagination!" The sea sparkled, and the houses along
Dune Road in Southampton glittered in the late August
sun. Mona was tired of the summer, tired of the Meadow
Club, tired of Southampton, tired and bored. She couldn't
wait to get back to Raffington's and Endicott's. "Now, look,
Solange. We'll get our paddles early and sit in the very first
row! I am going to have the Cadwalader chair if it's the last
purchase I *ever* make. What did you say? Fat what? Oh.
Don't forget, darling, September 8. See you! Kiss, kiss."

XOXOX

Selena arrived at Hellinikon Airport in Athens early in
the morning after having slept fitfully during the overnight
flight. She didn't really have a plan, just to find Neal and the
musicians from Wesleyan, and have fun for the remaining
two weeks before Labor Day. She wondered again and again
how things might have been different, how *she* might have
been different, if she had gone on the trip with Neal in the
first place. Had she learned anything at Endicott's? Was the
pain and disorder she had endured worth anything at all?
She felt too emotionally bludgeoned to think about it. Some
sun, some laughter, some sex with Neal was all she wanted
now.

After passing through customs, she took a taxi to the
Hotel Parakelo, which she knew was the jumping-off place
for the orchestra's tour of the islands. The manager was
helpful. He showed her a room full of baggage left behind
by ambitious packers who hadn't realized that lugging cellos
and timpani on the small island boats would preclude two
or three suitcases. He told her, after consulting a schedule
left with him, that the group would arrive back in Athens in
five days, and urged her to book a room. Selena persisted.

"Where is the orchestra now?"

Reluctantly, the manager told her: Mykonos; they would arrive in Mykonos that very afternoon. Selena inquired about the boat schedule to the island, learning that there was one sailing in two hours. With the help of the manager, she secured a reservation, and declined his invitation to breakfast on Tang and toast in the enclosed hotel dining room, going instead to the Plaka, the old city, and dining at one of its glorious outdoor cafes. The dry heat and translucent sunlight warmed and refreshed her. Under the majestic shadow of the Parthenon and the Acropolis, Athens was awakening, the proprietors of the small craft shops opening their doors. She stretched in the sunlight like a tabby cat, relieved to have put the unhappiness and difficulties of New York behind her.

After breakfast of strong Greek coffee and pastries, she hailed a cab and went to the docks in the old section, where she watched the bleached white ships undulate against the blue water. She didn't feel at all tired, but exhilarated and ready for adventure.

When she boarded, she found the boat crowded with Greek families, tourists of all nationalities, and a little clique of exotic-looking gay men, each wearing an astonishing quantity of gold jewelry. She spurned the boat's interior and sat on the deck, reveling in the beauty of the sea and sun as they pulled out into the brilliant blue. She pulled a cotton shirt and a headscarf from her bag, and wore them as protection from the sun. She couldn't remember another summer when she hadn't seen the sun or the ocean. Never again, she vowed silently. Neal was right. Never again.

The boat ride stretched for hours, and the sun was very hot, but Selena didn't mind. The sense of freedom on that wine-dark sea of Homer made her euphoric, nearly giddy. She felt young again. On deck, she shared a pita sandwich with two blond Austrian youths backpacking their way through Europe.

It was nearly dark when the boat docked. Mykonos, with its starched white buildings and brightly-colored doors, looked like a citadel out of the Arabian nights. How wonderful, she thought. Bidding good-bye to the Austrians, she walked into town and began inquiring about hotels. At last she found someone who spoke English, and after three telephone calls, reached the hotel where the Wesleyan Chamber Orchestra was staying. Her interpreter then showed her a poster of the orchestra's appearance affixed to a nearby wall. It was scheduled that evening at 9 p.m. in the town park.

Selena sighed excitedly. She'd come so far, and she'd found them. Her first thought was to ring Neal, but it was nearly dinnertime, and she didn't want him to see her looking like a soiled and sunburned deck hand. She booked a room at the hotel near the harbor for the night, collapsing gratefully in the whir of the air conditioning.

Though she was a fairly accomplished traveler, she began to feel jet lag, or more specifically, time-and-place lag. Her nerves were still electric, and she hadn't absorbed the fact that she had come half a world and an entire reality away from Endicott's. She got up and opened the single duffle bag she was carrying. Then she took a long, hot shower, thinking about how to approach Neal and the musicians, many of whom she knew from school. It mustn't seem that she was running after him. That would never do. After his behavior when they parted, she didn't wish to place herself in a weak position. The memory of the awful postcard also burned. But to say merely that she had finished her internship early, and decided to lark about before going back to school, seemed appropriate. Larking about was certainly Neal's bailiwick, and something he understood perfectly. She doubted he would question her further.

She chose a simple black knit sundress, and after getting directions from the hotel manager to the outdoor amphitheater where the orchestra was to appear, she walked to a little outdoor cafe on the waterfront, ordered dinner, and observed the anomaly that was Mykonos.

The white buildings, tiny dead-end alleys, and enchanting architecture were similar to the other islands, but there was a disturbing decadence here. The number of homosexuals she observed was extraordinarily high, and they looked for the most part wealthy and European. Among shops containing pottery and local fabrics, there would appear grotesque black leather outfits displayed on torsos of mannequins twisted in what could be interpreted as sadomasochistic poses. She thought of the men on the boat, and realized that the island catered to that clientele.

As 9 p.m. approached, she found her way to the outdoor square where the orchestra was already tuning up. She seated herself in the back of the arena, and listened as the concert began. How incongruous and lovely Mozart's Serenade sounded in this timeless and unusual setting! A soprano she recognized from campus sang a bel canto aria from Bellini's Norma. Unlike the local Greeks, the cultivated visitors understood the music, and applauded loudly. She looked about for Neal but didn't see him in the audience, so she simply relaxed and enjoyed the warmth, the night, and Mykonos.

When the orchestra had taken its final bow and the audience was trailing off to the adventures of the night, she suddenly saw him, a girl on each arm, walking down one of the far aisles. She stiffened in nervous anticipation. The girls were giggling, and Neal stopped in the aisle and began his version of the traditional Greek dance, arms uplifted and fingers snapping, to his companions' delight. When he was done, he bowed, they laughed, and he bounded up onto the stage, going up behind a violist and grabbing her around the waist. She tried to push him away, but he clung to her. Finally, she turned toward him and they kissed deeply. Then he put her viola into its case and they walked away, arms about each other's waists, Neal carrying the viola case.

Selena was struck dumb, paralyzed. She watched the little scene as one might watch a movie, seeing it unfold but not believing it, not really being there. Choreography. Direction. Lighting. She sat as if cast in stone. Anna had been right. Or had she? Selena rose, and in a trancelike state followed the retreating couple at a discreet distance. She didn't recognize the girl, who was pretty and blond. They wandered up a narrow alleyway, and Neal pulled the girl into a doorway and kissed her passionately. Selena was shocked, feeling like a voyeur, but she had to see this to understand it.

Eventually, the two arrived at an enclosed restaurant where lights covered with wicker gave an inviting glow. Most of the orchestra members had already arrived for what was obviously an ensemble late supper. Selena stood outside and watched with an appalled fascination. There was no doubt that Neal and the girl were having an affair. His behavior toward her was quite sexual, rubbing her inner thigh, looking deeply into her eyes, giving her food from his fork. Still she watched. Her only feeling was a kind of disassociated numbness. She didn't feel anger or betrayal, just a degree of wonder that she could have been so gullible. Had she traveled on this trip with Neal, it now would be she he was fondling, she he was sleeping with. But she had said no, so of course there was someone else to fill the position, provide for his need, fulfill his romantic fantasy. She laughed, and suddenly felt pity for the girl. Perhaps she was playing, too. Perhaps the girl wasn't as stupid as she herself was.

She walked away slowly through the warm night under the inky sky spangled with glittering stars, aware of the ghostly whiteness of Mykonos. She wandered about for a long time until she heard American music and laughter emanating from a cafe. She slipped inside and saw what appeared to be a woman, but was actually a young man in drag, outrageously costumed and made up, pantomiming to Mary Martin's "My Heart Belongs to Daddy." She, the only woman in the place despite its appearance, left as quietly as she had come.

She eventually found her way back to her hotel by finding the harbor, and fell into an exhausted and dreamless sleep, too tired, or too shocked, to cry. In the morning she rose, prepared herself quickly, caught the morning boat for Athens, and flew to Rome after a half-day's wait in the western wing of Hellinikon Airport. She didn't belong in Greece. It was time to go home.

Chapter 22

James the doorman, in his regal new uniform, stretched to his full height of 6' 3" and admired his reflection in Endicott's double glass doors. Though it was still warm, there was a hint of fall in the air, an electric charge of excitement. The fall auction season at Endicott's was beginning. How he loved it, seeing the long row of black limousines arriving in front of the venerable auction house. Ah! There was that pretty but slightly faded model for the *Sensuel* cosmetics line on the arm of a deeply-tanned, white-haired gentleman in an expensive Italian-cut silk suit. Wilbur van der Horst Carey, who lived in Monaco to protect his fortune from taxes? He thought so. As he opened the door and smiled at them, he knew he needn't worry about the rumors that she was about to be replaced in the man's affections. She'd be just fine, if the way he was looking at her was any indication.

Oh, yes, James knew his people, that he did. Next to alight were a punk rocker and the long-haired dish named Lily, she grabbing his arm. She frequently had hung around Endicott's earlier in the summer, and he had often seen her leaving late with Harris Tompkins—until last month, when almost everybody had disappeared.

But now it was auction fever again, and he just knew that today would be every bit as thrilling as the sale of the Duchess of Tudor's jewelry. The patrons were arriving early, and they were the rich and titled regulars. Who was that coming now? Yes, Mona Elliot, one of John Bunch's best. He extended his hand. "Mrs. Elliott—welcome back to Endicott's."

"Thank you *so* much, James," she twittered, and allowed

him to take her hand and kiss it. What a day! That fancy chair was about to be auctioned. Who'd have thought?

)O(O)(

In the executive offices, Sarah Dean had been in since shortly after 7 a.m. She had to speak to E. Martin Wunnicke before the sale, and before the press' fervid interest in the fall season waned. Time to ride the crest with the announcement of a new president. She watched carefully for activity in his glass-walled office, but there was none.

She checked and double-checked her work, the stacks of printouts. There was no written record anywhere about the illegal reserve program. All the department heads had been summarily debriefed and threatened with loss of their jobs, and the interns were gone. She'd done an efficient job, and she was quite ready to be rewarded. The last night she had spent with Wunnicke at her apartment, he'd been evasive, saying things "weren't entirely up to him," and "the board of directors has...."

She had simply stared at him in disbelief and said, "Of course it's up to you, Martin. You are the owner, the brains, the general. Did Napoleon let his officers tell him what to do? No! *You* decide, Martin." He'd merely nodded and kept on sipping an insipid martini.

)O(O)(

Simon, too, had arrived quite early. Today was the most important day of his professional life, and he meant to conduct it masterfully. He'd put his emotions completely aside in the weeks since Selena's departure and Freddie's death, and worked with a concentration and effectiveness he'd never achieved before. At the pre-auction reception, where the Cadwalader chair was on view to a select private audience, he had been superb, kissing every lady, commenting thoughtfully on every man's business dealings, selling the idea of The Chair—its cachet, as well as its provenance. He had mollified Grace Peabody, and persuaded her to visit his mother Camilla in St. Barths and leave the sale entirely up to him. He had negotiated smoothly with Wunnicke and Kazin, had held the vicious Sarah at bay, and had charmed the peculiar Alex Putnam into giving this sale the finest international publicity that Endicott's had ever had. He had coached Harris Tompkins again and again on his timing and wording about the chair. The failures and pain of his personal life didn't intrude, and he felt really quite effective and powerful, like the precision engine in his Mercedes purring into life, knowing exactly what to do and doing it superlatively.

※※※

Back on Park Avenue, James simply held the door open continuously as the stream of gorgeously dressed women trailing scents of exotic perfume, and powerful, wealthy men became a wave. He was astounded by the attendance, for the early viewing hadn't been overwhelming. Suddenly, a huge grey stretch limousine pulled up, and E. Martin Wunnicke and two other men alighted and went quickly past James. Was the man closing the limo door a bodyguard? He shook off the thought. Why would Wunnicke need a bodyguard? The arrival of Wunnicke's party seemed to send a new surge of energy through the crowd. On the sidewalk across the street, the celebrity watchers gawked and pointed. James smiled faintly. Oh, to be in the center of all this. It was sublime. It was New York! It was Endicott's!

Sarah jumped to her feet the moment Wunnicke and his

entourage entered, and hurried across the reception area. He was deep in conversation with the baron and Kazin, and without looking toward her, held up a finger admonishing her to wait. Herbert Kazin mumbled something, and the three men guffawed. Then Wunnicke turned his head, gave her a broad smile, and said, "Good morning, Sarah. Great day for a sale, don't ya think?"

She nodded unenthusiastically, and walked over to him. "Martin, everything's in order. I have Alex on alert for a personnel announcement." She looked at him meaningfully.

"Good, Sarah. You never let me down." At this, Baron Laszlo-Molinski chuckled. Wunnicke beamed. "Yes, there will be an announcement after the sale today." She nearly whooped for joy. "Join us in the executive dining room right after the sale. Oh, and bring Simon Haden-Jones along too, will you?" He turned to the other men, and she silently swore vile expletives to herself. Why did she have to bring him? As she turned to leave, Wunnicke said, "Spot well, honey. You'll look might pretty on that podium with old Harris." Again, the men closed ranks.

Really, Martin, she rankled as she turned to leave, you are quite, quite disgusting.

)(O)(

Harris Tompkins looked out his window at the swirl of people on the street, the line of cars, and heaved a little sigh. Another great auction. He looked into the mirror at the greyish pouches beneath his eyes, and tried to push back the fleeting thought that it was silly for a grown man to wear a tuxedo in the morning. Then he thought of Zubin Mehta, who was, of course, a patron of Endicott's. Didn't he wear a tuxedo during the day to conduct? Of course he did.

He guessed that his affair with Lily had run its course.

214

Was it his fault that Paul McCartney wasn't in New York this summer? Of course not. He sighed again at the obstinacy of the young, and for nights of ecstasy that had ended.

Practicing his best style and manner, he thought about the audience. Today would be a sensational triumph for him. He would play the crowd and attain a record price for the Cadwalader chair. And he'd met that pretty, divorced Bolivian tin heiress at the reception...who knew? And he was quite certain that he'd be officially named president soon, like his uncle before him. It was just a matter of time.

※※※

In the great auction salon there was a discreet rush for advantageous seats, and for the more conspicuous and important activity of seeing and being seen. For there was absolutely no doubt in anyone's mind that this auction was an Event. The auctioneer's mahogany podium gleamed, polished to a fine glow, adorned only with gold letters spelling "Endicott's." Floral arrangements bedecked the usually austere stage, lined in dull grey velvet to highlight the beauty of the antique pieces. It was 9:45, and the boards showing the various currencies had been set. Sarah Dean walked onto the stage to check the telephones. Bids on the Cadwalader chair were expected from London, Paris, Tokyo, Monaco, and Baghdad, and the lines would be kept open. She disliked spotting—watching to see that no bidders holding up paddles were overlooked—but it put her in front of the patrons at important sales and showed her importance. Two other spotters, girls from the executive office suite, would also be with her, behind Harris Tompkins, yet well away from the antique lots, which would be carried on by the practiced moving staff for their moment in the golden spotlight, then whisked away as the gavel fell.

XOXOX

Simon left his office and went down the stairs to the salon at 9:50. Although this sale and its brilliance were attributable to the Cadwalader chair, there were many other fine items in it, and he wanted to achieve the best prices for all of them to please all his clients. As he entered the back of the gallery, he was overtaken by a loquacious elderly lady, widow of a fabulously wealthy financier.

"Oh, Mr. Haden-Jones, I read the article on your apartment in *House & Garden* with such pleasure. So original." She beamed at him, and he had trouble thinking of anything to say. "Er...thank you, Madame. I hope you find something to please you in the sale."

"Oh, I will, dear boy, I will." She rushed off to her seat, for the event was about to begin. Simon sank back against a side wall, hoping to be left alone with the hundreds of details on his mind.

The lights in the salon dimmed, and an expectant hush fell upon the glitterati. Television cameras panned the stage as Harris Tompkins ascended to the podium, picked up his gavel, and said, "Good morning, ladies and gentlemen, and welcome to Endicott's sale of fine American furniture and decorative items." And so it began.

Mona Elliott, perched on her front-row seat, stared up at Harris Tompkins' chin, and whispered to Solange, "He's such a *darling* man. Doesn't he remind you of Connie?"

The first items offered were a pair of pewter candlesticks from the pre-Revolutionary War period, unsigned, but attributed to the Boston workshop of Paul Revere. After a desultory opening bid of $100, the bidding proceeded rapidly, and the candlesticks were hammered down at $750.

Simon breathed a great sigh. It was underway, and it

216

would go well, he could sense it. The energy of the patrons showed him quite plainly that they were in a mood to spend. Some of them, of course, would wait until the declining moments of the sale, after the highlight items had gone and audience interest had waned. Seasoned expert that he was, Simon always could spot these bargain seekers who wanted to "pick up a little item at Endicott's for a song." He understood and respected their desire.

He glanced up at the yellow oblong of light in the executive dining room, and could make out Wunnicke, Kazin, and the baron—Endicott's Holy Trinity, he thought with sarcasm. Turning his attention back to the podium, he realized that Harris was in fine form, and felt a wave of respect for his very special gifts. Damn the trinity! Why didn't they treat Harris better? He was pulled out of his reveries. The bidding had begun for a fine Chippendale lowboy, made in Philadelphia the same year as the Cadwalader chair. The gavel came down, the price well ahead of his estimate. Good, good, he thought. He left the salon by the main door and walked around back to where the antiques were stacked and lined up to be carried to the stage.

"Hi, there, Mr. Haden-Jones," said a man in loose overalls, grinning toothily. "Good sale, huh?"

"Yes, Rufe, it seems to be a very good sale."

The man and his partner dexterously lifted a cherry drop-leaf table, parted the curtain and carried it onto the stage, Rufe nodding cordially at Simon.

How professional they are, he thought. Then he saw the Cadwalader chair, still protected by a sheet. He worked his way carefully through the furniture and lifted the sheet. It looked fine and sturdy. The restoration was perfect. Was that a shadow of a spot on the damask seat? No—must be the dim light. He patted the chair's arm familiarly. Almost time, it's almost time. He smoothed the damask, and touched the hairy paws for perhaps the last time.

Gently replacing the sheet, he hurried back to the auction floor. The items were moving rapidly, and bringing more than his estimates—sometimes far more. He saw Arabella at the side of the salon, dutifully recording prices in a catalogue. Was this auction going to be a theatre of the absurd, like the Duchess of Tudor's jewelry? Sometimes the buyers' behavior simply defied logic.

He watched the items come up and be knocked down rapidly. Then the moment came.

"Ladies and gentlemen, the highlight of our sale today is lot number 186, a fine Colonial wing chair in the Chippendale hairy paw style from the Philadelphia workshop of Thomas Affleck, carved in 1770 by master carver James Reynolds. Known as the Cadwalader chair for the general who commissioned it. Shall we open the bidding at one hundred thousand dollars?"

There was an expectant hush in the audience, then a careering ripple of whispers. A paddle rose in the back, and one of the spotters whispered to Harris.

"I have $50,000, thank you." Another paddle rose. The back of the head was instantly recognizable to Simon as Hadley Brown.

"One hundred thousand, thank you." Two impeccably tailored blondes were manning the telephones. One spoke to Harris.

"We have one hundred *fifty* thousand. One hundred fifty thousand." Two paddles rose simultaneously, one in the front row. Was that Mona Elliott?

"Two hundred." Harris indicated Mona. "Two hundred fifty."

All of a sudden, there were five paddles and a bid being passed along by the telephone, until the bidding was in excess of one million dollars and gathering speed. Simon was tense, transfixed. Mona Elliott's bid of one million five hundred thousand dollars stood alone for what seemed to Simon like an eternity. Harris raised the gavel. "Are you all through? The bid is one million five hundred thousand dollars, going once...."

Suddenly, a new bidder whom Simon couldn't see entered and set off a new wave of bidding from Mona and Hadley Brown. There was excited activity from the telephone spotters as the foreign bidder continued. When the bidding reached two million dollars, there was a collective gasp from the audience. The intensity in the room was palpable. No one seemed to breathe. Finally Harris said again, "Are you all through? The bid is two million dollars for this fine chair, two million, going once...going twice...." He raised the gavel.

Simon couldn't believe his eyes! Another bid had come in by telephone and there was a simultaneous bid from Mona in the front row, and now the bidding was off again, escalating to two million five hundred thousand in an instant. Simon felt as if he were in suspended animation. He picked up a catalogue and looked quickly at the pre-sale estimate, confirming that it was $700,000 to 900,000. And they were at two *million* five hundred thousand? He felt that he, and the entire room with him, had crossed from reality into some mad zone where money was simply a toy, or scrip, or as mutable as a paper doll, whatever you made of it. A fleeting thought told him that that figure must translate into billions of yen, trillions of lire....

When Harris' gavel was about to fall, Mona Elliott's paddle rose again, tentatively, and he could hear her say, "Two million seven." Harris acknowledged her bid and there was another collective gasp, then complete and utter silence. Simon watched the spectacle as if it were an incomprehensible drama set in outer space.

After checking with the telephones, the two blondes gave

barely perceptible shakes of their heads to indicate that the overseas buyers had dropped out. Sarah, the other spotters, and Harris surveyed the crowd anxiously. Mona had grabbed her friend Solange's arm, and was wiggling with excitement.

A smoothly professional Harris Tompkins said quietly, "The bid is two million seven hundred thousand dollars... two million seven hundred thousand dollars for the one and only Cadwalader wing chair. Are you all through?" He raised the gavel slowly, slowly, watching the audience carefully for any sign of continued bidding.

At the last possible second, Hadley Brown stood up. Stood up! It wasn't done, and Simon grimaced. He held his paddle like a weapon, and yelled loudly, "Two million nine hundred thousand...two million *nine* hundred thousand dollars." The TV cameramen panned to the late bidder.

Harris repeated the bid and looked down at Mona, whose face seemed literally to have cracked. She spoke sotto voce to Solange, then stared at Harris stonily, willing herself not to betray emotion. He looked directly at her. "There is a bid of two million nine hundred thousand against you...two million nine hundred thousand going once...." Mona fumbled in her purse for a handkerchief, which she brought to her lips.

Two million nine hundred thousand going twice...." All eyes on the stage were riveted on the front row where Mona Elliott sat frozen.

"*Sold!*" The gavel came down firmly. "To number 163 for two million nine hundred thousand dollars." To release the tension, the audience began to applaud.

Hadley Brown had won, then, but on Simon's terms, not his own. Simon could imagine the disbelief of Grace Peabody when he telephoned her. As for himself, he was in shock. He glanced up at the window of the executive dining room to see Wunnicke standing there, smiling broadly. He caught Simon's eye and gave him an avuncular thumbs up.

The sale of the Cadwalader chair had indeed gone well.

"Well, well, Simon, you certainly outdid yourself this time." Wunnicke insisted on patting him on the back, a gesture Simon found particularly distasteful. A weary but proud Harris Tompkins fixed himself a drink at the sideboard. Sarah was drinking tea with lemon, and Simon asked the obsequious waiter for coffee.

"How'd the TV interviews go?"

"Quite well, sir," Simon answered. "The prices were sensational, as you know, and the reporters were very interested."

"Two million nine hundred thousand for that chair of yours. I'll be goddamned." Wunnicke shook his head. "I think congratulations are in order, Simon."

"It was just luck, just some very interested and tenacious bidders," Simon said.

"Oh, I don't know about that." Wunnicke smiled slyly at the baron and Kazin. "Let's sit down. We have some company business to discuss."

Sarah seated herself discreetly near Wunnicke. Simon sat across the table. My turn, Sarah thought, my turn, my turn.

"We've been giving a lot of thought to a replacement for Walter Everest, and in the process we've decided to reorganize things a little and add a new position."

Chancellor of Ancient Chairs? Sarah thought, looking at Simon contemptuously. That explains why he's here.

"We've created a new job of executive vice president, and we're going to ask *you* to fill it." He turned and looked Sarah in the eye.

"What?" She went white. "Executive *vice* president? To whom?" She was struggling for control.

"Well, this is what we've decided. In the best interests of

Endicott's, we are naming Haden-Jones here as our new president."

"What?" said Sarah and Harris simultaneously. Sarah's teacup clattered into its saucer, and she began to gasp, at last rising, excusing herself, and running from the room.

"*Me?*" Simon asked. "But I'm an...."

"You'll do a wonderful job for us." Wunnicke stared at him.

Simon looked at Wunnicke and Baron Laszlo-Molinski and Herbert Kazin, but he did not see them. Nor did he hear Harris throw more ice cubes into his Scotch. He saw Freddie in his hat, laughing and greeting friends at Raffington's, then Freddie in a metal drawer with a tag on his toe. He saw his beautiful Selena in her little black hat, gazing up at the stars in his Mercedes, then Selena running from him in terror down the corridors of Endicott's.

He saw his little son in his pram, holding a rattle. He saw his life as it had been, saw it clearly, and he knew somehow he had arrived at match point.

When he finally spoke, he was scarcely audible in the elegantly appointed private dining room.

"Thank you for your offer, Mr. Wunnicke. I'm honored. As you know, I've devoted most of my professional life to Endicott's, and I've loved it. But...I must decline."

"*What?*" said an astonished Wunnicke. "Did you say 'decline'?" Anger began to cloud his face.

"In fact, I'm resigning, effective immediately."

There was a stunned silence. Harris smiled to himself.

"What do you *mean* you're resigning?" Wunnicke shouted. "Has Bronte's made you an offer?"

"No, sir."

"Then what the *hell* will you do?"

Simon took a deep breath. "I haven't the least idea."

Epilogue

Simon sat in his darkening apartment, watching the hues of the sunset go from gold to rose to umber, nursing a Scotch and trying to clear his mind. He only heard the traffic going by in the street and the bleat of horns and swoosh of the buses starting up through the filter of the air conditioner's hum. He nursed the drink and tried to think, but inside his head was a kaleidoscope of impressions and emotions.

Although he had no idea how he had managed to say what he had to Wunnicke—it was completely unplanned—he knew without a doubt that it was the right thing.

The right thing. He'd never confronted the idea before except in the abstracts of philosophy. He'd always assumed that what he did was right. It was right to work hard. It was right to think of others. It was right to honor your parents, and to be true to your word. It was right to be faithful.

At this thought, he got up and walked across the room to pour himself another Scotch, neat. He looked out the window at the lights coming on in the apartments across the avenue, and wondered why things had changed so much.

It was right to tell the truth. The truth—that elusive value that seemed to pass through the prisms of everyone's perspective differently.

He sat up throughout the night, dozing occasionally, drinking occasionally, but unsettled.

What would my father do now? The questions came unbidden. He didn't have to ask what Selena would do, with the certitude of youth and inexperience. The questions kept returning....

As dawn broke, he knew what the truth was, and what he would do about it.

Precisely at 9:00 a.m., he called police headquarters and asked for Detective Mallozzi. "That would be third precinct, downtown." Simon scribbled the number, then dialed it.

He repeated his question to the operator, and a phone buzzed. "Joe Mallozzi." The voice was curt, harried.

"Hello, this is...this is Simon Haden-Jones, Lieutenant," Simon said hesitatingly.

"Who?" Mallozzi asked.

"Simon Haden-Jones, of Endicott's Auction Gallery. I met you when I identified my friend a few weeks ago."

"Ah, what name? Oh, the jumper we looked into as a possible? What was his name?"

"Trowbridge, Freddie Trow...I mean Trosper."

"Oh, yeah, yeah. How can I help you?"

"I want to report some...irregularities at Endicott's, and I need to know how to go about it," Simon said slowly.

"What kind of 'irregularities'?" Mallozzi asked.

"Well, I guess it would be...something like price fixing, or fraud?" Simon said uncertainly.

Mallozzi let out a low whistle. "Are you sure?"

"I'm sure," Simon said without hesitation.

"Okay," Mallozzi said. "I don't know if this will be state or federal jurisdiction, let's see...I dunno. But I'll get you a name. What's your number? I'll call you back."

Simon gave him the number and slowly hung up the receiver.

He breathed in deeply, and stretched. He knew without even thinking it that his life, as he had known it since his childhood, was over.

XOXOX

Much later, years and events, Simon Haden-Jones, on his first vacation from his teaching position at the University of Leeds in England, went to Florence to see Michelangelo's *David*. He was looking for the Galleria dell' Accademia, taking in the beauty of the architecture and the streets.

He had found himself to be a good teacher, was becoming better, and art history was a natural for him. But he had more to learn, much more, and he dedicated his vacations to seeing the museums and art treasures of Europe.

As he turned a corner, he saw a figure ahead, walking in a certain way, with long dark hair bobbing. He stopped suddenly, startled. Then he quickened his step to overtake the hurrying figure, reaching out to touch her shoulder.

The End

ORDER FORM

Fax orders: (401) 846-1774. Send this form or a copy.

Telephone orders: (401) 846-7592

Web site orders: www.newportliterary.org

Mail orders: Newport Literary Society
               31 Division Street
               Newport, Rhode Island 02840

Send e-mail to: newportlit@yahoo.com

Please send the following books:

_____

_____

_____

_____

Name: _____

Address: _____

City: _____State_____

Telephone: _____ E-mail: _____

Sales Tax: 7% for items shipped to Rhode Island addresses.

Shipping: Please add $6 per order for Priority Mail postage and handling, $4 for regular mail.